THE
CATCH

Books by Mick Herron

The Oxford Series
Down Cemetery Road
The Last Voice You Hear
Why We Die
Smoke & Whispers

The Slough House Series
Slow Horses
Dead Lions
The List (A Novella)
Real Tigers
Spook Street
London Rules
The Marylebone Drop (A Novella)
Joe Country
The Catch (A Novella)

Other Novels
Reconstruction
Nobody Walks
This Is What Happened

THE
CATCH

Mick Herron

Published by
Soho Press, Inc.
227 W 17th Street
New York, NY 10011

Library of Congress Control Number: 2019952884

ISBN 978-1-64129-234-4
eISBN 978-1-64129-235-1

Printed in the United States of America

10 9 8 7 6 5 4 3 2 1

THE
CATCH

They came for him at dawn, just as he'd feared they would. But instead of using the Big Red Key so beloved of SWAT teams—the miniature battering ram that reduces a front door to matchsticks—they entered in civilised fashion, and when he opened his eyes they were in his bedroom, one regarding him as if he were a carving on a tomb, and the other examining a photograph on the dressing table that showed Solomon Dortmund when young, a mere fifty or so, holding hands with a woman the same age, and whose quiet smile for the camera could pull a drowning man ashore. Surrounding this photograph were a pair of beloved relics: a hairbrush and a small velvet drawstring bag, an inch square, containing three baby teeth and an adult molar. This was disturbing, but when you appropriate a man's life without his blessing, you leave his family treasures where you find them.

"Two minutes, John. You'll be on the pavement in two minutes."

"Could you make it five?" His voice was scratchy, and badly dubbed. "I could do with—"

"Two minutes. Richard here will keep you company."

And then it was just John Bachelor and this man Richard, a large, shaven-headed thirtysomething with thick-framed spectacles, who gazed at him unsmiling. It seemed unlikely that they would arrive at an odd-couple friendship in the time allowed.

When he shifted, a sour smell escaped from the blankets.

"You couldn't pass me my trousers?"

Richard patently regarded this as either rhetorical enquiry or statement of fact.

There is a peculiar humiliation in dressing in front of a hostile stranger, particularly when one's body is an increasingly rackety collection of limbs attached to a soft, baggy frame, and one's clothing a medley of items purchased at bargain prices. Bachelor's corduroy trousers were shiny at the knee, and his shirt had a faint spray of blood on the collar. His own, it's important to note. Even so, it was a relief not to be standing in his briefs in front of someone whose own physical decline, if already etched in outline beneath his dark blue suit, had yet to be framed and hung for all to see.

Squeezing his feet into socks produced the kind of hyperventilation that running up stairs once triggered.

He stood up. "I need to, ah . . ."

Richard affected incomprehension.

"To piss, man. I need to piss."

John could see him thinking about it—actually thinking about it. When did we grow so hard? He was too young to be former-Stasi.

"It's your two minutes," he said at last. "But leave the door open."

Of course. In case John used the precious moments to retrieve the handgun from the toilet cistern, or assemble the miniature helicopter secreted beneath the floorboards.

It was an old man's bathroom, with an old man's shaving gear on a shelf, an old man's mirror on the wall, and an old man's reflection residing there, so Bachelor ignored it, raised the toilet lid and pissed. Lately, he had been dosing himself with Solly Dortmund's sleeping tablets, a large number of which he had found in the medicine cabinet housing that same mirror. Solly Solly Solly. Old men have trouble sleeping, and medication was an obvious recourse. But if he had been prescribed pills, why were they still here? Solly had been a hoarder, but to collect sleeping pills spoke of building himself an escape hatch, equivalent to a handgun in a cistern, or a miniature helicopter. In the end, of course, he had needed neither, which meant that his trove remained intact for John to plunder. Which, in turn, meant side effects: John's urine had acquired a metallic odour, and he wondered now if it were drifting out through the open door, assaulting Richard's nostrils. He hoped not, and at the same time tried to convince himself of the upside to the worst happening: that he need no longer await its appearance.

"Time's up."

I know, John thought.

He'd known it for a while.

They took him not to Regent's Park, the home of the Service, but to Marylebone High Street. Richard drove. The other man sat in the back with John. He looked to be in his fifties, a man with some years' secret experience behind him, and not unused to collecting the wayward and conveying them somewhere like this: an empty office above London's favourite bookshop, its white walls newly decorated, its carpet squares not yet bedded in, so that the joins could be seen crisscrossing the floor, as if marking out a board game. For the players, there were two chairs, dining-room variety. There were no blinds, and light streamed through the windows while the city yawned. It was all very—John strained, momentarily, for the precise word. It was all very alarming. If they'd been thugs, he'd have known he was in for a kicking. But they were suits, which suggested a more vicious outcome. In other circumstances, he'd have been wondering what he'd done to deserve this. As it was, he knew full well.

"Sit there."

Not an invitation.

He took the chair indicated, and the older man sat in the other, a clean metre or so between them. The younger man took station by the door. There could be no mistaking this for anything but what it was: the interrogation of a wrongdoer. It would be sweeter, quicker, if he simply confessed and saved everyone time. Whatever it is you think I've done, I've done it. Can we go home now? Though he had, of course, no home to go to. A fact which lay at the heart of what it was he'd done.

"So, John. John Bachelor."

"That's me."

"Yes, John. We know it's you, John. Otherwise we'd look a right pair of nanas, wouldn't we, collecting someone who *isn't* John Bachelor this bright summer morning. So you're who you are, and we're us. Richard there, you already know his name. And I'm Edward. Eddie to my friends. Very much Edward to you."

"Edward it is."

Edward sighed. "I recognise that you're eager to cooperate, John, and that's going to save a lot of inconvenience. But don't waste breath on things that don't need saying. Which is a polite way, John, of telling you not to speak except to answer questions." He clasped his hands. "If you want to hear a less polite way of being told that, go ahead with the irrelevant interruptions. Clear enough?"

John nodded.

"Nods aren't going to cut it, John. When I ask a direct question, I'm going to need to hear words coming out of your mouth. So once again, was that clear enough?"

"It was."

"That's better." Edward smiled, though not in a realistic way. Edward, thought John, was less of a suit than he appeared. Edward might have put on jacket and tie at some ungodly hour this morning, but that was as far as it went.

Edward unclasped his hands. Even at this distance, John was getting a hint of a fragrance he'd first detected in the car; a robust, peppery smell, from a soap that doubtless came in masculine packaging. He imagined waxed paper wrapping a weighty disc, its surface embossed with an heraldic design. All of this was offset by his awareness of his own body odour, never alluring first thing in the morning, and worsened by fear and interrupted sleep. His stomach churned repeatedly. His chin felt rubbery. His whole body, when you got down to it, was a sad disappointment. But Edward was speaking again:

"Before we start, there's something you should know. When an action like the one we are currently undertaking is mandated, a certain amount of administration occurs. Acceptable limits are signed off on. Mission parameters defined. What I'm saying, John, is that the worst-case scenario has been budgeted for, so I'm not looking at reputational damage if things turn sour this morning. Nor is Richard. I thought it might help if you were in possession of that information. There's no need to acknowledge your understanding. You don't get to sign a waiver or anything. What happens, happens."

John thought, All this, really? He'd been expecting some kind of bureaucratic retribution, but this melodrama? An empty office, a sinister warning? And yet it was working, because he was scared.

Edward nodded, confident his words had hit home. He tugged at his lapels, straightening his suit jacket. "So let's get down to business, shall we? Benny Manors, John. What can you tell me about Benny Manors?"

Well, okay. He hadn't been expecting that.

John Bachelor was Service, had been all his adult life. So by any fair calculation, he ought to have been comfortably settled by now: not a Desk, obviously—reaching Desk level required drive, ambition, contacts, dress sense and at least a glimmer of sociopathy—but enjoying cubicle status and a pension. Instead, he was on the margin; downgraded last year to "irregular," which meant part-time, with an accompanying reduction in salary. When he'd complained to HR, the rebuff had been comprehensive. If the Service operated a zero-hours contract, it ran, that's the level he'd have been pegged at, so he might as well stop trying to make waves. Even making ripples was above his pay grade.

They were barely aware, to be frank, that he was in the pool at all. Putting the phone down after this illuminating chat, he'd felt as if everything had become a little looser: the buttons on his cuffs, his shoelaces, his sense of self. What made it worse was its inevitability. His life trajectory resembled one of those puzzles in the Saturday papers: *What is the next number in this sequence?* He'd been counting down to zero for years.

And it was salutary how a few poor choices could scuttle you, information it would have been useful to have had at the outset. There had been a house once, he remembered that much, and he was pretty sure it was still standing, and that his ex-wife still enjoyed the breakfast bar, the bedroom extension and the patio that had been intended to both improve their quality of life and increase the property's value. The latter had almost certainly happened—he'd never heard of a property in London *losing* value, short of it burning down—but was no longer of direct relevance to him, a matter that, for the avoidance of doubt, had been clarified in a courtroom. There'd been a pension too, until he'd taken advantage of the draw-down opportunity to bury a huge chunk of it in his former brother-in-law's foolproof investment opportunity, a mirage of such IMAX proportions that he genuinely couldn't recall the details of the product at its heart. Skateboards for mermaids? Feline Zimmer frames? Some such fucking thing. And meanwhile here he was, wrong side of sixty, catering to the Service's has-beens. A milkman.

"Milkman" was a term of contempt, of course. Agents were joes; desk jockeys were suits. They were different ways of fighting the same battles, and while each had been known to look down on the other, like characters inhabiting the same Escher staircase, they shared a commonality neither would deny; a sense of purpose. A milkman, though, had failed to make a mark in either endeavour, and could be trusted to do no more than his weekly round: touching base with the pensioners and the walking wounded; those who'd served behind whatever lines had been drawn in their day, and now required support in their evening. Not that all were elderly, or, if the truth mattered, entirely honourable. Solomon Dortmund, though, had been a jewel. Had it ever occurred to Solly to view John Bachelor with disdain, it was a thought he'd have smothered in its cradle.

And so, in the way these things have of occurring, John had been living for the last eight months in Solomon Dortmund's apartment, two flights up in a proud brick building off the Edgware Road. It wasn't large, but it was comfortable. Solly's choice of pictures hung on the walls, and Solly's umbrella lived in a stand by the front door. And Solomon had died of a heart attack in the bedroom, and John had done right by him, he was morally certain of that—arranged the funeral, invited the old man's comrades, put money behind the bar. Had spent an evening in the company of strangers, all of whom remembered Solly fondly, and all of whom had wondered who he, Bachelor, was, precisely? Not a relative, surely. That "surely" contained a wealth of ethnic certainties. So no, John wasn't a relative; was, rather, the son of a man with whom Solly had done business in the long-ago. The nature of this business was left vague, and those who had known that Solly, for all his gentle manners and kind habits, had once performed certain services for a certain Service, had nodded wisely, and left it at that. And afterwards John had returned to the flat, Solly's keys in his pocket, Solly's umbrella in his hand.

It had been a hard winter, with inches of snow even in London, and it had been a relief to find himself behind a closed door, the weather locked out in the cold. Relief has a way of becoming habit. The tasks John performed after Solly's departure had not included informing his department that Mr. Dortmund was no longer on the planet, and it was surprising how easy it was for a bureaucracy to overlook such trivia. Left to its own devices the Civil Service is a *perpetuum mobile*, and accordingly the arrangements for Solly's well-being remained in place: his bills paid, his pension gathering dust in his bank account. John never laid a finger on Solly's money, obviously. That would have been wrong, and difficult. But John laid his head on Solly's pillows, and laid his body down on Solly's bed; he rested his feet on Solly's coffee table while planting his arse on Solly's sofa, and he cleaned out Solly's fridge and pantry without his conscience uttering one chirp. He was doing no harm. It was this or sleep in his car: who could afford London rents on a three-day-week salary? And he'd run out of friends among the living. So it was Solly's generosity he relied on, and Solly's roof that sheltered him through the rest of that hard winter, and a wet spring, and a record-breaking summer. If there was a downside, it was the anxiety that fizzed in the background like white noise. Unbroken luck was an unknown factor in John's life, and waiting for the fracture to happen wore at his nerves. Hence his use of Solly's sleeping pills.

This, or most of it, provided a wealth of explanations for his current situation: sitting on this chair in this room, with Edward being fierce at him.

Benny Manors, though, had never entered his mental picture.

"**Benny Manors**, John. What can you tell me about Benny Manors?"

Bringing him back to the present.

"Benny, well, Benny," he said. "What can I say? Benny's one of mine."

"We know, John. Sole purpose of visit, as they say at passport control. Little more detail, eh?"

John searched what others might refer to as their

mental database, or perhaps Rolodex, if they were of a certain generation. For John, it was more akin to opening an ancient filing cabinet he'd long stopped keeping in alphabetical order. Some of the papers were scribbles on envelopes. Benny Manors. That was a name he'd shoved to the back, in the hope he'd not have to deal with it again.

"Because I've been looking through your Ts and Cs, John. That an abbreviation you're familiar with? Doesn't mean tits and cooze, if you were wondering. No, it means terms and conditions. As in, of employment. You remember that, John, the job you do? The one you're paid for? Remind me what they call you?"

"I'm a retirement needs evaluation counsellor—"

"You're a milkman, John."

John nodded.

"And what your Ts and Cs very eloquently state is that, in that role, you make contact with your clients, bare minimum, once a month. Which is handy for me, as I'm keen on having a word with one of those clients, the aforementioned Benny Manors, and on account of the terms and conditions of your employment, I'm in the happy position of knowing I'm talking to someone who's had contact with Benny in the last four weeks. Bare minimum. Meaning that within the next two minutes I'm going to have a much clearer picture of our Benny's current whereabouts than I do now. So that's nice for me, isn't it, John? Nice knowing I have you to paint that picture for me."

It must indeed have been nice for him, living in that state of certainty, though it was a little less comfortable for John Bachelor. Because John hadn't laid eyes on Benny Manors in well over two years.

It was one of those things, one of those moments. You meet someone and right there, in the first flush of new acquaintance—forget about taking time to be sure; sometimes you can feel it in your marrow, no hesitation—right there, in that first moment, you think: well, this isn't going to fucking work, is it?

He'd already had Benny Manors's history down pat. Say what you like about John Bachelor, but he did his job, or at least, turned up prepared to do his job. It was only after that preliminary stage that things might go wrong, as with, for example, Benny Manors. So yes, he had Benny's number, and it wasn't what you'd call prime. Because Benny was a louse and Benny was a chancer. One of those who definitely fell within the category "not entirely honourable." What Benny had been, when you got down to it, was a crook. Breaking and entering, though he'd discovered a sideline when a venture into a likely looking property had yielded an interesting collection of Polaroids among the loose cash and petty jewellery, Polaroids Benny

had amused himself with a time or two before it occurred
to him that while the starring role of Old Man in a Nappy
had evidently been taken by the gentleman occupier of
the recently burgled house, the two young women sup-
porting his act were definitely not his wife. And thus
Benny had learned that some stolen property enjoys a cash
value above and beyond what it might reach down the
local, because the elderly gentleman proved expensively
keen to reacquire possession of his souvenirs rather than
have them, say, appear on the internet. It was Benny's
pleasure to make the old man's dream come true. Well, his
latest dream. Going by the evidence, earlier versions had
already been taken care of.

So that was Benny Manors, and that became his career:
housebreaking a speciality, but with an eye for the unusual
item. Careers have been built on lesser talents—soap stars,
presidents, novelists—and he might have happily continued his course without interruption had he not come to
the attention of a Service talent spotter. Every so often
Regent's Park found itself in need of an amateur, largely
to avoid any fallout should the situation at issue turn
unexpectedly professional. So, Benny Manors having
dropped onto its radar as a snapper-up of unconsidered
truffles, the Service pressganged him into carrying out
an after-hours excursion into the premises of a certain
Eastern European gentleman resident in Knightsbridge,
whose diplomatic status technically put him off-limits,

but whose private life remained of surpassing interest regardless. Anyway, long story short, the situation did in fact turn unexpectedly professional, with the result that Benny Manors, in what turned out to be the briefest Secret Service career since George Lazenby's, rather than acquiring any useful information acquired a permanent limp instead, courtesy of the Eastern European gentleman's domestic help, which was rather more energetic than the average Knightsbridge household required. Benny, and what remained of his left leg, were deposited in a dumpster just outside the postcode. This was felt by Regent's Park to be coincidence rather than deliberate slight, but who knew?

Anyway, never let it be said that the Service turns its back on those wounded in its employ, even when the employ is unofficial, and especially when the wounded suggests appealing to the court of public opinion, or Twitter, as it's now known. Which is how Benny Manors came to be on John Bachelor's books: not exactly a retiree, and not exactly a shining example of one who's given all for his nation's benefit, but a man with a limp nevertheless, which he hadn't had before the Service came into his life. It took all sorts, John supposed.

And that first meeting had been at a pub near King's Cross, he thought—he remembered the occasion, but it wasn't like he'd be treasuring it on his deathbed or anything. So let's say King's Cross, and let's say the usual dark panelling and Fuller's beer-mats, the usual door to the gents as easy to negotiate as a tiger trap. Benny let John buy the drinks, because that was the way of the world. And Benny let John explain what their relationship was going to be before sinking that ship before it left harbour.

"Once a month? No no no. No no no no."

Seven nos. Even allowing for the double negative, he was definitely giving this the thumbs down.

At this time Benny would have been late forties. No longer as lithe as he'd been in his youth—who is?—but given that much of his particular youth had been spent worming through windows technically too small for him, he'd had a higher bar to fall from than most. So he wasn't in terrible shape, damaged leg apart—it had required metal pins, several of them; he was a special case at airports, Benny Manors—but all in all, he wasn't too bad a picture of a late-forties man, also allowing for this being his choice of meeting place, mid-afternoon. *Homo saloon-barensis*. He had wiry gingerish hair and a two-day stubble. And his suit was classier than the pub they were in, not to mention the beer he was drinking—Newcastle Brown Ale? John hadn't been aware anyone actually drank that. He thought the bottles were just kept handy in case a fight broke out.

He followed up his Lear-like string of negatives with an unnecessary clarification. "Once a month isn't going to work for me."

"I don't make the rules."

"See, that's the sort of thing that gets said by people who spend their sorry little lives doing exactly what they're told."

John Bachelor's life at the time wasn't as sorry as it would become—he was still on a full-time salary—and he didn't enjoy the description.

"What exactly is your problem, Benny? What makes it such a chore to have a quick face-to-face round about pay day?"

"Did I say it was a chore?"

"You're not making it sound like a pleasure."

Benny was drinking straight from the bottle. He took a good long pull without taking his eyes off John, then said, "This leg I'm carrying round. I didn't break it climbing out a window. I had it shattered, bespoke-like. By two bastards doing an impression of a pair of brick walls."

His accent was plain and unvarnished, but *bastards* had a flatness to it. His file hadn't included deep background— Benny Manors was evidently unforthcoming with his personal information, possibly an occupational wariness— and he hadn't been important enough to warrant legwork, if you didn't include the job carried out on his actual limb. So John didn't know but wondered if Manors wasn't city-born at all, but hailed from up country. Would explain his choice of drink. But he was still talking:

"So the way I see it is this. You pay the compensation as agreed, and you stay out of my line of sight. That clear enough?"

"If I don't see you, you don't get the money, Benny. It's as simple as that."

"Yeah, right, but, that's not actually simple at all, is it? What that is is downright complicated. Because I don't plan to spend the rest of my natural being wherever you want me to be once a month simply to collect what's owing to me. The dosh goes straight into my account, right? It's not like you're carrying round an envelope full of fivers."

There had been a time when that was precisely what milkmen did—carried round bags of money. But this way of doing things, reliant as it was on the honesty of all parties, had been brought to an end back when Michael Jackson was King of Pop.

"So there's no actual reason for me to have to be anywhere, is there?"

John Bachelor wasn't used to this attitude. Most of his clients were glad of the company: a friendly face, some kind words. The opportunity to talk about the old days, when they'd done whatever they'd done that had brought them into his ambit. Mostly, this had involved acts of courage rather than petty burglary. Mostly, they were better men and women than Benny Manors. Snap judgement, but this didn't seem an uphill battle.

It occurred to him that he didn't want to spend the rest of his own natural having this conversation once a month.

"So what I suggest," Benny was saying, "is that you just turn in your monthly report saying yes, all's well, Benny's fine. And instead of us actually having a meeting, you can have a lie-in. How does that sound?"

"Again, Benny, what's your problem? It's ten minutes out of your busy schedule. Which, let's face it, must have gaps in it these days. I mean, it's put a crimp in your burglary career, right? Having a leg like an overcooked noodle."

When he got up from the floor the barman was already in Benny's face, telling him to bugger off sharpish, no mistake. Benny was shaking his head, not disputing the marching orders, but ruing the punch he'd delivered. A little more precision, John's teeth might have made a pretty necklace. As it was, he simply had a bloodied nose.

"Misunderstanding," said John. "Just a misunderstanding." He made to pick up his stool.

"Don't you worry, sir, I'll see to that."

He cleaned himself up in the gents, assured the barman there was no need to trouble the police, and left. It was brighter outside than he'd been expecting, or maybe that was just his head ringing unnecessary changes. When was the last time he'd been hit? Must have been at school. On the other hand the next time might be on the cards already, because here was Benny Manors again. But he had his palms showing, indicating he wasn't about to throw another punch. The limpy git.

"You asked for that," was what he said.

Actually, he might have had a point.

"But I'll tell you how I plan to make it up."

And he did.

"So tell me, John, where's our Benny? And what's our Benny up to?"

"Well," John said, and toyed with the possibility of leaving it at that. Looked at philosophically, while Edward's questions remained unanswered, the possibility of John's being able to answer them remained alive, as did John's future and, indeed, John himself. Not that he seriously thought these two were going to kill him. On the other hand, if Edward didn't look precisely like someone who'd killed people before, he did look like someone who'd received news of other people having been killed with perfect equanimity. Which was enough of a prompt to allow John to get to the end of a sentence: "Well, he moves around a bit."

"He does, does he? I'm assuming you mean residentially speaking, John. Because the information I have regarding Benny Manors is that his mobility is seriously compromised. Not about to launch into a rumba without warning, is he?"

"He doesn't like to be tied down," said John. "Feels the need for flexibility."

"Again, I would cite the construction work done on his leg. Except I suspect you're going to tell me you're speaking metaphorically, aren't you? You're going to tell me Benny Manors fancies himself a free spirit, just one Volkswagen camper van short of a trip to Kathmandu."

"Well . . ."

"Or put another way, what you're telling me, John, is that the address currently on file for Benny Manors—the file you're in charge of keeping up to date, I don't need to remind you, except it seems I do—that address is not actually his address, which would explain why he's not there now, and hasn't been for some considerable time. Would I be right in summing up the situation in that fashion, John?"

". . . Yes."

Edward sighed.

John said, "It's a delicate business, looking after the Service's old-timers. I have to take into account their needs, their situations, their psychological—"

"Bullshit."

Well, precisely, thought John. Their psychological bullshit.

"Benny Manors isn't some traumatised asset still having nightmares about his weeks behind the Wall. He's a small-time housebreaker and blackmail artiste who, if he hadn't had his leg smashed up on a one-night stand for the Park, would almost certainly have had his dick caught in someone else's mousetrap by now, except that way we wouldn't be paying for his cornflakes. So when he told you about his *needs*, you should have told him about his obligations. Among which was keeping the Service informed of his whereabouts. And that would be you, John. In this very minor instance, you represent the Service."

From over by the door, a snorting noise reminded John that Richard was still in the room.

"And yet, you have fucked up. Fucked up, John. And while that is nothing new in your long and unillustrious career, it puts me in an embarrassing situation, and that, let me make clear, *is* something new. And to make it even more humiliating, I now find myself in the demeaning position of looking to you to extricate myself from this embarrassment."

". . . Yes."

"You still haven't got the hang of this, have you? That wasn't a question."

Edward leaned back, which struck John as mildly dangerous. These chairs weren't made for cavalier posturing. But mostly what he was thinking was, this wasn't as bad as he'd feared. If he was required to do something, that meant being allowed to walk out of this room in order to do it. Moreover, whatever this was about, it wasn't about Solly. It wasn't about him living in dead Solly's Service flat, which—the shock of a dawn collection notwithstanding—was far more crucial to John's well-being than any minor fuck-up he might have made regarding Benny bloody Manors. Because if the Solly business came up he not only wouldn't have the flat any more, he wouldn't have a job either. And this wasn't a world waiting with open arms to find future prospects for John Bachelors. It was a world waiting to crush them under its unforgiving heel.

"So, let's start with the confession. Because there's always a confession, John, we both know that. Let's start with why you let Benny Manors wander away like a kid at a fairground, without ever putting it on a report."

He could have lied, but John Bachelor had told enough lies in his life to know when one was likely to haul him out of the mud and when one would step on his head. So he told the truth: about that first meeting in King's Cross, which had ended with Benny punching him in the face and him falling off his stool with a bloody nose. And about what Benny had said when he'd joined him outside in the sunshine; about how he planned to make it up.

"And this would be money, wouldn't it, John?"

"Yes."

"Because it always comes down to money with a certain type of citizen."

John couldn't immediately tell whether the type in question was Benny or himself. He supposed, though, that it didn't really matter in the circumstances.

What Benny had suggested was that they arrive at a little understanding. The understanding would be in the nature of fifty quid a month, payable the day after Benny's monthly stipend reached his bank account.

"I'm getting paid to keep quiet, when it comes down to it," Benny had said. "And now you're being paid for exactly the same thing. And this way I get to keep my privacy intact. More secure, see? And as you're in charge of my welfare, that should suit you down to the ground."

"I'm supposed to file a report."

"Well, there's nothing to stop you doing that, is there? I mean, how detailed do these reports get?"

Details, well. John had details down to a fine art. "Nothing to report" was a not uncommon entry.

"Can't stand here all day, John."

And so he'd said yes, and that was how it started, and pretty much how it finished too. *Going to need your bank details, John. Not like I'll be turning up on your doorstep once a month with the cash. Whole idea is, I get to do my own thing here.*

Edward was shaking his head in disbelief by the time it got to this part. "John Bachelor," he said. "John Bachelor. You would have lasted exactly two seconds in the field. Any field. Walk into a fucking *corn*field, you'd last two seconds."

Richard spoke for the first time. "He made one payment only, didn't he?"

John nodded, then remembered his instructions. "Yes."

"And then you were on record as having received money from him, and after that he didn't have to pay you sod all."

"The art of the bribe, John," Edward said. "Once you've made your catch, you can keep the rest of the bait for yourself. And you're telling us you've had no contact with Benny Manors since?"

". . . That's right."

Another sigh.

He could hear traffic building up; cars and taxis ferrying people to their places of work. The cafés up and down the High Street would be welcoming breakfast customers, and the homeless in the doorways would be stirring, knowing they'd be moved on soon. The day, which was going to be a hot one, was starting to flex its muscles. John had forgotten what he'd had planned for the day ahead. Everything looked different now.

Edward was staring at him, and he had the sense that there was unspoken communication going on between him and Richard. As if they were checking cues, awaiting a prompt. Whether it arrived John couldn't tell, but Edward began talking at last, and it went on for a while.

"Now, I'm going to explain the facts of life to you, John. I'm aware that some of them may have come to your attention in the past, but it's always good to have a refresher, isn't it? And the important thing you have to remember is, your balls are in a vice. And I'm operating the vice, John. And if I ever decide to take a rest from operating that vice, which I won't, but if I ever do, young Richard there is going to step in for me while I do whatever it is I've decided is more important than operating the vice in which your balls are trapped, and he is going to operate that vice in my stead, and let me tell you something about Richard, John, Richard is a disappointed man. About ten minutes ago in our terms, which translates to half a year or so in young Richard's, he was very much the rising star. Diana Taverner's favourite son type of thing. Man most likely to. Instead of which he found himself stepping into the most enormous pile of shit, as a result of which he is no longer anybody's favourite son, and is in fact as popular at Regent's Park as a red-headed orphan. This close to Slough House he came. This close." The helpful gesture illustrating this was a thumb and a finger, so close to touching no daylight slipped through. "The only reason he was spared that fate is Lady Di wanted to deny Jackson Lamb the fun of dismembering him. But that lucky escape aside, Richard's disappointment is a real and living thing, John. What you might call organic. So Richard finds himself in the position of having to feed that disappointment, John, feed it so that it doesn't devour him instead, and what he likes to feed it is anybody he can. Which right here and right now, John, would be you. Let me know that you're keeping up."

"... Yes."

"Good. So this is what's going to happen, John. You are going to find Benny Manors for us, and you're going to hold him in place until we come and collect him, and that is going to happen swiftly. Otherwise you are going to discover what a vice round your balls feels like, and you're not going to be discovering that while hiding away in a cosy little flat off the Edgware, John. Because yes, John, we're aware you've been living in a dead man's trousers. Using a dead man's electricity and gas and water, and for all we know hocking a dead man's treasures in order to satisfy whatever unnatural cravings keep you awake at night. Porn or booze, John, I don't care which. All I care about is you finding Benny Manors, failure to do which will turn my full attention to the clamping properties of this vice we're discussing. For example, I might decide to take a closer look at whatever caused Solomon Dortmund to have a heart attack last winter, and without wanting to give away spoilers, John, I'm very likely to decide that it was you. I mean, it's the old *cui bono*, isn't it? Who profited from Solomon's demise? That would be the man who's taken over his life and trappings."

So much for this not being as bad as it might be, thought John.

"In summary, I really wouldn't want to be your balls, John. Neither one of them. But on the upside, your way out of this mess is clear, yes? You simply do what you're told." He stood abruptly, and the chair toppled onto the carpet with a muffled thud. "Richard here will be in touch soonest. Check on your progress. We'll give you a couple of days, John." He cracked his knuckles. "A couple of days. Then I'll start getting irritable. And you don't want that."

The list of things John didn't want had grown exponentially this morning, but he could agree that Edward growing irritable was likely to be included. It didn't seem worth corroborating this, though, so he didn't waste his breath on a reply.

As they watched him weave up Marylebone High Street, looking not all that different from others starting to appear on the streets now—those who had places to go and things to do—Richard said to Edward: "I think we motivated him."

"That was never going to be the problem. Someone as shit-scared as Bachelor's easy to motivate. No, the major difficulty is the usual one when you're using shoddy tools. Are they up to the job? Or will they fall apart in your hands?"

And as he was watched doing his weaving, John Bachelor thought: whatever's going on here involves several layers of fuckery. He was a milkman, for god's sake. If they wanted to put the frighteners on him, all they had to do was threaten to sack him. So there was something going on here, more than appeared on the surface. Not that that altered things much. Whichever way you looked at it, he was going to have to find Benny Manors.

Biggest puzzle of all, though, was: How come they couldn't do this by themselves?

First thing first, he had a drink. Early doors by anyone's reckoning, but sometimes you skip the niceties. Back in Solly's flat, sitting by the window, he watched the morning get a grip on itself while he drank an inch of peach brandy, discovered at the back of Solly's sideboard and saved for an emergency. The first gulp burned the way the first gulp does any time of day, though the peach flavour added a hint of breakfast. Good to maintain a schedule. And while he was doing that he ran through his mental records on Benny Manors, which took zero minutes. It wasn't as if he knew the man's haunts or habits; they'd had exactly one meeting, and that hadn't gone well. And if Edward and Richard hadn't managed to find him with the Park's resources at their disposal: well. Why did they expect him to accomplish what they couldn't?

In this whole sorry mess, he was holding only one card that he could see.

He knew who Richard was.

Because their stories had collided in the past. Or brushed against each other, rather, the way a pass might be made at a railway station: information delivered, received, in the briefest of exchanges: an envelope swapped, a password muttered. So he knew this much: that Richard's name was Richard Pynne, inevitably demoticised to Dick the Prick. And how he knew him was, Dick the Prick had stolen what should have been the crowning jewel of John's career.

For once, just once, he'd had a glimpse of the limelight. After the death of one of his older clients, a list had come into John's possession, a list of supposed sleeper agents. The details were probably written down somewhere, but the upshot was that John himself—John Bachelor, milkman—recruited an agent, Hannah Weiss. Not a high-flying operative, no Red Sparrow, no Modesty Blaise, but a mole of sorts, allowing the Service a glimpse into the workings of its German counterpart: not a bad day's work, if he said so himself. And he did say so himself, but to little avail; Hannah was taken away from him and placed in the care of one Richard Pynne, Lady Di's favourite and a noted high-flyer, who for some reason was thought a better choice to run a minor domestic op than clapped-out John Bachelor, who'd never done anything more complicated than carry bags and tell bedtime stories to ancient spooks.

Funny thing was, he'd heard rumours since that the whole operation, small beans as it was, had gone tits up, with young Hannah turning out not to be a double at all, but a triple; not so much allowing the Service a glimpse of the workings of its German counterpart, but the precise inverse. Which meant Richard had in fact done him a favour, even if it hadn't felt like that at the time. London Rules: always be a fair distance from a fuck-up. And if it had been a rumour when he'd first heard it, it had obviously calcified into fact since, for here was Richard, so far from the seat of power that he was manning the door while someone bigger and crustier than he was put the screws on that clapped-out milkman.

You could call it karma. Or just one of life's *fuck you*s.

The brandy was gone. He contemplated a second glass, but experience suggested that a second had a way of becoming a fifth, so instead booted up his cranky Service laptop and accessed his client files. There Benny was, in all his muted glory: the history of his brief career in the Service, the slightly longer history of his previous known activities, the address in Wandsworth which was clearly no longer current, his bank details . . . bank details? The man was out there with a bank account, money going in, money coming out, and those clowns couldn't find him with the whole of the Hub at their disposal? Unless it wasn't. That possibility had been nagging at him from the start, when they took him to a vacant safe house instead of the Park. Unless this pair were on a frolic of their own. So he considered that for a while, and came to the alarming conclusion that it made little difference. Even if they were off-reservation, that didn't render their threats harmless. They knew about the flat. They knew enough to screw him up badly.

And unless he could think of a way of getting round that, he had no choice but to find Benny Manors.

So he hit the pubs round King's Cross. What else was he going to do? He asked about his old friend Benny, had Benny been in?, and received blank looks. One place he was convinced had been the pub where it started: this was where he'd been sitting when Benny punched him in the face. There was the door to the gents it had been a struggle to navigate. But he had the same sensation an hour or so later somewhere else, and besides, what difference did it make? Nobody had heard of Benny here, there, or any of the places in between. They weren't establishments where one punch thrown several years back was still talked about. There'd been punches since. They blurred together.

And another problem was, going into a pub and asking questions, it was de rigueur to buy a drink.

Drunks and pigeons: there are homing instincts. In fact— one of the random thoughts that flitted through John Bachelor's brain at two in the morning, when it occurred to him that he was back at Solly's, with no recollection of getting there—in fact, it would be interesting to get a pigeon drunk, to see whether this improved its homeward flight time. But that thought only lasted as long as it took him to crawl into bed, where the ceiling rotated like a fan in a black-and-white movie. He hadn't found Benny Manors; hadn't even found anyone pretending they knew Benny Manors. If Benny Manors had suggested King's Cross as a convenient meeting place, it was only because Benny Manors hadn't wanted John to know where a really convenient meeting place might be, such as wherever it was Benny Manors actually hung out. And as things stood, the only pointer he had to Benny's whereabouts was that, on their one and only encounter to date, the man had been drinking Newcastle Brown Ale. That notion circled John's head in the opposite direction to the ceiling, making him nauseous. He was too old for this. And even when he'd been young enough for this, it had lacked what you might call glamour. He slept at last, or managed a kind of sleep, which felt more like a ride on a broken Ferris wheel. When he regained consciousness, he felt abandoned rather than rested. And the usual morning stocktake yielded no happy balance: he'd spent nigh on a week's salary greasing conversational wheels, and his mouth felt like a ferret's timeshare.

He stumbled to the shower. It was still early, way too early, but the glimmer of an idea had broken on him while he was riding that wheel, and although its only real attraction lay in the absence of any alternative, there was a slight possibility that its light might guide him home. He was probably still drunk, after all. And it would be foolish not to take advantage of the fact.

So not long afterwards he was loitering near a gym in north London, head pounding, eyes bloodshot, but upright, showered and dressed, which, given that it wasn't yet half seven, suggested from a distance that he was a productive member of society. More productive members had jobs to do: while he waited, a van dumped bundles of newspapers outside a shop, their headlines variations on the same theme, that the waves made by the recent suicide of an American billionaire in his prison cell were still breaking shore this side of the Atlantic. The man had been a sex trafficker, and a well-connected one. A particular connection was mentioned by name in 48-point font. Not a happy day at the Palace, John surmised.

He was spared further contemplation of this odious pairing by the appearance of the woman he'd been hoping for.

She emerged from the gym with the air of one for whom the world has been on hold while she'd been otherwise occupied, a gym bag over her shoulder, her hair tied back. She was wearing sunglasses, possibly to avoid being recognised, but more likely because it was already bright, already warm. John wished he were wearing shades himself. At the very least, they'd have helped disguise his bleary appearance. But too late now. She'd already spotted him.

"John Bachelor," she said, making little attempt to hide her contempt.

"It's important."

"It had bloody better be."

She was all in black: black sweats, a black hoodie. Only her trainers offered colour: black too, but with a crimson band. Her hair was wet, and though she was still recognisably Diana Taverner—Lady Di—First Desk of Regent's Park, he'd never seen her looking like this before: like someone who had a life. He suspected few people had. He wondered how many of them dared boast of the experience.

"How did you know to find me here?"

This was disingenuous. She liked it known that she did a ninety-minute early morning workout three times a week, and this was the most expensive place near her private residence. So he'd got lucky that this was one of those mornings, but everyone deserves the occasional break.

All he said was, "I didn't. Not really."

"Do I need to press a button?"

Which she'd have in a pocket, and would bring the Dogs running. That was all he needed, second morning in a row: to be tossed into someone else's vehicle and taken somewhere he didn't want to go. "No. Please don't."

She pushed her sunglasses up her nose. It was an oddly endearing moment, which was not something he'd ever expected in her company.

"There's something you need to know about," he said.

For a second or two, it seemed she'd dispute this. To inform him that it was unlikely he'd ever be in a position where there was something he knew that she didn't, yet. He remembered their being in a pub together once, at a wake for a dead colleague, and she'd outlined his role in life, the full ambit of his responsibilities. *It's hardly* Tinker Tailor, *John. You wipe their noses, feed their cats, and make sure they're not blowing their pensions on internet poker.* The kind of summation he might have made himself, though he'd have pretended there was humour in it. But instead of heading down that road again, she said, "Okay, you've got my attention. For twenty seconds. Let's hear what your problem is, and then I'll decide whether it's worth this gross intrusion of my privacy."

"I'm being played."

She rolled her eyes. "You're being 'played'? *You're* being played? Seriously, John, that's a three-word sentence, and it's only the middle one isn't ridiculous. Who do you think is trying to play you? An amateur percussionist?"

"One of them's Richard Pynne."

And this landed, he could tell.

She took a moment to change her bag from one hand

to the other. "Pynne? What would Richard Pynne be doing on the streets? He was reassigned from Ops. I think he's in charge of the stationery cupboard now."

"And someone called Edward. Biggish guy. Fifties. Wearing a suit, but looks like he's done heavy lifting in his time."

"It's a big organisation. We could have any number of Edwards on the books."

But this name too had triggered recognition. He could tell.

"But here's me using up your twenty seconds. What were this pair after? Just the bullet points."

"They want me to find Benny Manors."

"Manors, Manors, Manors. Oh, Manors. Well, they went to the right person, I assume. He's on your round, isn't he?"

"Yes. Except . . ."

"Except what?" She halted, and John had walked a step on before he noticed and halted too. "Except you've mislaid him, yes?"

"He's not exactly one of my lock-ins."

"If he's on the payroll, he touches base. It's not a complicated principle."

"He hasn't always kept his appointments," John said.

"But when I check your records, and I will, I'll find the monthly reports all in order, right?"

"I keep clean records."

"I'm sure you do. Okay, leaving that aside, this pair, Pynne and this Edward, are looking for Benny Manors, and they come to you. What exactly do they have on you that makes them think you'll do their bidding?"

And here was the gamble.

Out in the sunshine he made his confession, trying to make it sound like an administrative oversight, one of those things that happens at work, the way a pad of Post-its might find its way into your briefcase. Everyone's wound up living in a dead colleague's flat, surely? That was the tone he was aiming for, all the while reminding himself that he had little alternative. Either he gave himself up, here and now, or someone else gave him up, soon. And at least this way he was bringing something to the table, besides his own misdeeds. At least this way he could spin it as gently as possible. And he could still tell himself he was halfway to getting away with it, until he clocked her expression.

There were rumours she'd turned a man to stone once, with the power of her stare. Except, John now realised, they weren't rumours, they were interdepartmental memos. He could feel his limbs solidifying. He'd never leave this spot: they'd have to fix a plaque to the pavement explaining who he'd been and warning people not to chain their bikes to him.

"You do realise," she said at last, "that I could sack you right now for what you've just told me."

"Yes, but . . ."

She waited. He'd sort of hoped she'd come up with a *but* all by herself.

"But I can make it right. This pair, they're up to something. I can help you find out what."

"And in return, I'll what? Forgive you your sins?"

"Maybe give me another chance."

"Jesus, John. How many second chances do you need? You've had more lives than a cartoon cat." She glanced at her gym bag, as if contemplating whacking him with it. If he was the cartoon cat she imagined, he'd go a funny shape on impact, before shaking himself back to normal. "Your time's more than up."

She meant the allotted twenty seconds, he hoped. But it was possible she was taking a longer view.

Taverner fell quiet. John had an urge to speak, to fill the silence with more apology, but had the sense not to. The hole he'd dug was deep enough. At last she said, "Pynne no longer has Hub privileges, which means he'd have to make a formal application to run a trace. So the reason they came to you is, they want to find Benny without anyone knowing they're trying to find Benny."

"Except me."

"Without anyone important knowing they're trying to find Benny," she amended. "Or maybe there's more to it. Manors, if memory serves, was a two-bit blackmail artiste before some idiot recruited him for an op. He's been feeding off the Service tit ever since. But if a pair of our own are looking for him, it's likely because he's reverted to type and has something on them. Blackmailers don't change their spots. So he's currently gone to ground, and they want the nearest thing to a friendly face to bring him into the open. And that would be you."

"I'm not sure Benny thinks of me as a friendly face."

"Well, that shows good judgement, but whether he likes you or not is beside the point. The fact is, he knows who you are. He's not going to fear the worst if you show up, he's just going to think his pension's at risk." She pursed her lips and thought some more. "Okay. If a couple of Park people are running rogue, I want to know why. So I'll tell you what I'll do, John. I'll find out where Benny Manors is. And then you find out what he knows that's so important to two of my agents."

"And what do I do if they come back before then?"

"I'm sure you'll think of something, John. When it comes to saving your own skin, you generally do."

Which was as much of a compliment as he was likely to receive from that quarter. Finding the nearest café, he drank a large Americano, black, while thinking about the peach brandy back in the flat. This didn't make him an alcoholic, he decided. The probability that he'd drink some once he got home did, though. It was another bright morning, everybody looking happier as a result, John Bachelor excepted. He didn't think he'd improved his situation. On the other hand, he'd prevented Edward and Richard from spoiling it first, so maybe that counted as a victory. Something to warm his cockles, when he ended up sleeping on a pavement.

And when he got home, Richard Pynne was in his sitting room, Solly's sitting room, holding a ceramic cat, plucked from Solly's collection of knick-knacks.

"You have a key," John said, redundantly.

"I have a key." He nodded towards the other chair. "Do sit."

John sat.

"You've been out early."

"Places to go, people to see. You know how it is."

"And is any of this activity connected with, ah, with the matter in hand?"

"With finding Benny Manors?"

Pynne nodded.

"Yes. Yes, it was."

"Good. So where is he?"

"I said it was connected," John said. "I didn't say I had a definitive answer yet."

"I'm here to remind you of the, of the *urgency* involved."

"Nobody said anything about it being urgent," John said.

"That was implicit in our interview."

"I know who you are," John said. "You're the one took over Hannah Weiss."

Pynne's face darkened. It made him look younger, somehow; not an angry man, but a sulky boy. He let the cat fall to the floor. The carpet was thick enough that this didn't matter. "That's none of your business."

"You're like me," said John. "Peaked early. You get used to it. You just have to not care that other people are doing so much better."

Pynne looked round. "I haven't sunk this low," he said. "An old man's flat. An old man's *life*. And none of it yours, not really."

"Can I offer you some peach brandy? It's surprisingly moreish."

"You need to focus on the task in hand," Pynne told him. "That's what I came to remind you. Where's Benny Manors? Everything else, that's background static. Find Benny Manors, and do it quickly. Or all this, crappy as it is, comes to an end."

"What did Benny do?" John wondered. "Or what did you do that he found out about?"

"Task in hand," Pynne repeated.

"You're not as threatening as Edward. You need to work on your menacing skills."

The younger man stood, and John's heart thumped faster. But all Pynne did was stoop and collect the cat. He put it back on its shelf, then stepped back to admire the collection as a whole, the bits and bobs that accumulate during the years spent standing still. "I don't need to be menacing," he said. "All I need do is make one phone call. And then you're back sleeping in your car. If they don't lock you up."

"I never slept in my car," John said, though he'd come close. And there'd been snow on the streets then, and would be again before long. The winters rolled round faster than they'd used to.

"Just find him." Pynne put a hand on his shoulder; took a brief grip on his collar. "You've got one more day."

And then he left, leaving the flat's front door wide open, so John had to follow after him and close it.

It seemed a childish form of aggravation.

But the whole encounter had lacked point. True, his heart had been thumping for a moment, but only because a large young man had got to his feet unexpectedly, and John—let's face it—wasn't built for confrontation. Still, though, why had Pynne bothered coming, if that was all he had to offer? He'd have mused on this more if his phone hadn't rung. Private number, the screen read. He was prepared for Taverner's voice before he answered.

"Your missing friend."

"Let me guess," he said.

Taverner paused.

John said, "He's in Newcastle, isn't he?"

"... Where?"

"Newcastle upon Tyne."

"What the hell are you on about? No, he's not in New-castle upon Tyne. He's in Seven Dials. Or that's where he's been using his plastic."

John wished he'd kept his mouth shut.

"Are you still there?"

"You don't have an actual address?"

"You're supposed to be a spook, John. A clapped-out, useless one, true, but still a spook. Try to get in touch with what's left of your ambition."

John Bachelor's main ambition was not to wind up homeless.

Di Taverner said, "Have you got a pen?"

"Sec."

He found one on the little hall table, next to Solly's landline, which still rang occasionally. Cold calls; wrong numbers. There was a neat little notepad too.

Lady Di read him a list of places where Benny Manors's credit cards had been lately, and rang off without wishing him luck.

John Bachelor went to find the peach brandy. It had been a long morning.

Oliver Nash was there when Di Taverner made that phone call. Head of the Limitations Committee, he was a fre-quent presence at the Park, above and beyond the regular

meetings his role demanded; was so much in evidence that
one or two voices had been heard wondering if he were
nursing romantic feelings for Lady Di herself. When these
musings reached Taverner's ears, which they did with an
immediacy suggesting the use of either advanced surveillance technology or the supernatural, she made it be
known that random executions were her preferred means
of dealing with gossipmongers. She was famous for many
things, Diana Taverner, but not her sense of humour. The
wonderings ceased.

And anyway, Nash's romantic yearnings were directed
less at her than at the workings of the Park—a career
bureaucrat, he could still find hidden within himself the
super-spy of his adolescent daydreams. And who was to
say that hero wasn't still in there? There was certainly
space for him, with room left over for an astronaut and an
engine driver, Nash's ongoing diet having proved dogged
rather than successful, like an English tennis player.

"So Bachelor came to you in person," he now said.
"Something of a surprise?"

"Yes and no."

"That's how mediums and other charlatans work. Pro-
viding answers with maximum bandwidth."

She said, "We'd expected Pynne to be the one pointing
him in the right direction. But Bachelor had other ideas,
and doorstepped me instead."

"Resourceful type?"

"More the cowardly lion. It was a damage limitation exercise. He seems to think I was unaware of his living arrangements. But we always allow for a degree of improvisation."

Nash nodded, as if he knew full well the way operations were handled, but it didn't seem as if his heart were in it.

"Don't worry, Oliver. We'll get the desired result."

"It depends on what you class as desirable."

"Now now. Queen and country."

"I suppose so," he said. As always, he had his smartphone in his hand; as always, he couldn't conduct a conversation without it attracting his attention. At present, a morning headline filled his screen. The dead American sex trafficker. He shook his head. "Filthy business."

"That's often the way, I'm afraid."

"I have nieces," he said. "Teenagers. Young teens."

"Sometimes you have to focus on the bigger picture," she explained.

Seven Dials. He seemed to recall an Agatha Christie with that in the title, which suggested he might encounter the usual suspects in the usual places: spinsters in the kitchen, colonels in the bar. Maybe a vicar or two in the library. As it was, Monmouth Street was just another London thoroughfare, cheerful in the sunshine and grubby round the edges, and peopled by the usual young, the usual old, the former acting like they owned the place while the latter actually did. He'd made a list of the places where Benny Manors had paid bills, frequently enough that it could be assumed that this was his, well, manor. John Bachelor recognised the territorial instinct. With all the freedoms London offered, its natives tended to stick to their own warrens: local haunts, local habits. If Manors had drunk here last night, the night before, he'd drink here tonight, too.

Which meant John was early, but that was better than being late.

He could kill time any number of ways—there were shows to see, galleries to visit—but shows cost a fortune and galleries were full of art, so cafés and bars it was. The first was Italian: reasonable coffee, a stool by the window. Benny had been here last week for breakfast. It was only morning, but felt like evening already. John had been up hours. And had work scheduled that obviously wasn't going to happen, so spent twenty minutes on the phone while his coffee cooled, making apologetic calls to clients he wouldn't be seeing. He liked to think he made a difference to their lives—made them feel important, or at least, remember that they'd once been so—but the equanimity with which his absence was greeted caused him to wonder. On the other hand, little about his current situation didn't cause him to question something or other. If he remained in one place long enough, he'd doubt himself out of existence.

And there was money to think about; there was always money. He'd saved on rent these past eight months; on the other hand, what he'd saved on rent he'd spent on drink, to quell the anxiety caused by the means he'd adopted of saving rent. Life was a series of loops, each smaller than the last. He did sums on a scrap of paper: he wasn't carrying that much debt, if you didn't count the credit cards, but his bank balance didn't look healthy. Where did money go? If he could only answer that, he'd be free to live a happy, healthy life. Where did money go? All he did was eat and drink. He bought another coffee at London prices while he pondered. If he was kicked out of Solly's flat—when he was kicked out—best-case scenario, he'd be looking at a room in a multi-occupancy hovel, unless he could work his way round Diana Taverner first. She was the key. He had to work his way round Diana Taverner, which meant he had to be really, really lucky. He sipped his coffee, stared out of the window, and Benny Manors walked into the café and sat two stools along.

It was like being on a safari, or visiting a wildlife park, when you realise a lion has just wandered into view. First of all, don't scare it away.

Secondly, don't get eaten.

Instead of wasting time not believing what had just

happened, John went with it, putting the scrap of paper in his pocket and gazing out of the window: sunshine and strangers, tourists and taxis. Meanwhile Benny had a newspaper and was turning to the back pages. Cricket. He hadn't looked John's way. And without his having placed an order, food was brought to him: scrambled egg and sausages. Definitely his regular breakfast haunt.

He ate unhurriedly, a man on his own timetable. John tried to match his carefree manner, addressing his coffee with what he hoped was insouciance, and thus slopping some onto his jacket. He fumbled for a napkin and dealt with the damage. By the time he'd finished, Benny Manors, instead of studying his paper, was staring at John, not bothering to hide his disdain. "That is one cack-handed approach to a cup of coffee."

"It just sort of splashed out."

"I'm trying to remember your name, and failing. But I know who you are."

"John. John Bachelor."

"Are you following me, John Bachelor?"

"I was here first."

"This morning, maybe." He also picked up a napkin, and dabbed his lips with it. "How worried should I be?"

John, nodding towards the paper, said, "About the Ashes? Very."

"I remember last time, I flattened you. You going for the double?"

"I just want to talk."

He seemed no older, John thought. Sure, it was only a couple of years, but they'd been the sort of years that can wreak damage—look what they'd done to the country, not to mention John himself—and Benny had weathered them like months in spring. He was wearing a cream linen jacket over a white shirt and blue chinos, and might have been about to head off to a relaxed office, a creative consultancy or whatever. With a bouncy castle in the lobby, roller skates in the corridors. As he hadn't seen him come in, John hadn't clocked how Benny was walking, whether the limp was better. But he didn't appear to be using a stick.

"So," Benny repeated softly. "Should I be worried?"

"Probably. But not about me."

"So how come you're the one who's here?"

"Maybe it's your lucky day."

Benny Manors said, "You don't look like anyone's idea of a lucky day." He glanced down at his plate, and speared half a sausage with his fork. "They called you a milkman, right?"

"Yes, well. There's a lot of jargon."

"But you were never important. Messenger boy type of thing. Despite your advancing years."

"Yes, well," John said again. He was going to have to work on his conversational stopgaps. "Reason I'm here, a couple of real spooks are looking for you, and they're doing it off the books. What that's about is anybody's guess, but it's unlikely to be because they had a sudden hankering to buy you scrambled eggs."

Benny gave an unamused smile. "Good job I can afford my own, then."

His phone rang.

Without taking his eyes off John, he answered it. The voice on the other end was a tinny whistle, but John could make out a name, almost: *It's Daisy*. Davy? No, Daisy.

Benny said, "Five minutes," and disconnected.

"Best guess," John said, "is that you're back to your old game. And that you've got hold of information you think is worth something."

"I'm trying to eat my breakfast."

"And I could walk away and let you. But that won't help you in the long run. These guys, the ones looking for you, they'll find you. Even I found you. How hard could it be?"

"I'm guessing you had help."

John blinked, which was probably a giveaway.

Benny returned to his breakfast.

John said, "Okay, I had help. And you know what? That emphasises that you're in a hole, Benny. Enough of one that you've got two spooks looking for you on their own time, and the Service putting a pin in you because they want to know what's going on. So I could walk out of here now, but all that would mean is, you'd lose your one contact on Spook Street. Your one chance to have someone to stand behind when things get complicated. Which they will do."

"Is that your hero speech?"

". . . I don't follow."

"It sounded like something you've been practising. A hero speech. You know, so everyone, or me anyway, will realise you're the good guy."

"I just don't want to be kicked out of my flat."

John hadn't realised he'd been about to say that. It revealed him as weak, as frightened. In some situations, that was the right move, but Benny Manors was a black-mailer, the last man on earth to be moved by someone else's predicament. Which made it strange, the look on his face now. He laid down his knife and fork. His mouth turned serious; his eyebrows clenched. "You're going to be kicked out of your flat?"

". . . It's possible."

"Boo fucking hoo."

He got working on his final sausage.

John nodded: yeah, okay. That was not unexpected. He had about an inch left in his coffee cup, and drained it, wondering what his next move should be. He didn't really have one. He could call Taverner; he could call Richard Pynne. He was leaning towards the latter: if Pynne and Edward were working this under the bridge, then chances were they planned harm to Benny Manors. Right now, that sounded good.

A young woman had entered the café and was standing behind Benny. He didn't look round when she spoke. "Stuffing your face again."

"But also working."

"Yeah, right. In what way exactly?"

Manors tilted his head towards John, without looking at him. "Told you they'd make contact."

The young woman turned John's way, regarded him speculatively. It was possible that she was not overwhelmingly impressed. "Him?"

"Regent's Park's finest," said Benny Manors, and laid his cutlery down again, this time on a clean plate. "You wanted proof. Here's your proof. They wouldn't be trying to stop me if they weren't worried."

John tried to look like he knew what was going on.

Mostly, though, he was just happy to learn that he wasn't the only one who was worried.

To say that the business with Hannah Weiss, when he'd found himself handling an agent who was spying on the Park rather than for it, still rankled with Richard Pynne was tantamount to suggesting that Tom might remain a little pissed off with Jerry. Before and after snaps of his career resembled those you'd get of a seventies kids' TV presenter pre- and post-Yewtree, and if he hadn't been exiled from the Park—assigned to Slough House, the spook equivalent of Devil's Island—he was *persona non grata* on the Hub, which was where the power plays went down and where he'd assumed his future would be spent. Richard had been Lady Di's go-to boy; she'd been grooming him for bigger things. So he'd foreseen a numbered desk there: a Second, at least. Instead, he was now taking up space in the press liaison office. Which meant that, sitting on a visitors' bench in the Park's central lobby as Diana Taverner approached, it was hard not to feel bitter about what might have been.

But hard, too, not to quell the spark of hope lately ignited. He'd fallen from grace but here he was all the same, chosen for an op, and who'd have had the sign-off on that but Lady Di herself? So maybe he'd done his penance, and was ready to be welcomed back into the fold.

"Richard."

"Ma'am."

"What have you got?"

He'd hoped for a *how's it going?*, a *good to see you*. But he could manage the business tone as well as anyone.

He said, "Bachelor's made contact."

"You're sure?"

"I tagged his collar. We know exactly where he is. And Manors's phone is in the same room. A café on Monmouth Street."

"Good."

She'd never been lavish with her praise, exactly, but

the monosyllable sounded niggardly to his ears nevertheless.

"And how did Entwhistle do?"

Entwhistle, who'd introduced himself to Bachelor as
Edward, was ex-army and now one of the Dogs, the Service's internal police. A lot of recruitment was done from
the armed forces. It was possible they enjoyed the prospect
of coming the heavy with those known to the army as "the
funny buggers."

"About how you'd expect," Richard told her. This didn't
appear to be detailed enough, so he added, "He put the
wind up Bachelor all right. But I could have done that
myself."

"Of course you could."

"It's not like it would have been an uphill—"

"Richard, you're not without your talents, evidence to
the contrary notwithstanding. But you're not hard-man
material. I'm not saying you don't have the bulk. It's more
that you lack the . . . gravitas."

"Ma'am."

"Entwhistle played his part, you played yours. I'm
grateful for the assistance. I hope it didn't drag you away
from anything important?"

Ha bloody ha.

"Then thank you."

She turned to go.

"Ma'am?"

"What is it?"

"Something you should know. Bachelor recognised me. My name, anyway. Entwhistle said too much, so Bachelor knows who I am."

She half turned back. "Yes, Richard. We wanted him to know who you are. Why do you think you were chosen for the job? Now, do carry on."

And then she really was away, out of the lobby and heading for the restricted areas, where Richard Pynne had once wandered freely but which were now closed to him, and thus looked like any other gated paradise.

After a minute or so, he made his way back to the press liaison room.

They'd left the café when an influx of tourists threatened their privacy, onto the street's morning sunshine, then round a corner and into a wine bar. It wasn't open for business, but Benny shouted a greeting to a man polishing the woodwork of the curved counter, and pointed to one of the booths against the far wall.

"Quiet business meet, Yol."

This seemed to be okay with Yol, or perhaps just so commonplace it wasn't worth taking issue with.

They settled themselves on a banquette.

"What kind of name is Yol?" John wanted to know, but Benny just stared at him, so he didn't pursue it.

Daisy appeared to be used to such encounters, or at any rate unfazed by them. She had hair that was probably normal really, but was currently feathered with strands of purple, or it might be indigo. Startling, either way. She looked a quarter John's age, and yet was old enough to have a career, which was also startling. It was a wonder his eyebrows weren't constantly raised these days: a perpetual state of mild shock. Hair apart, she looked the way all young people looked now, which was a lot healthier than young people had looked back when he was one. Maybe they had better role models. That or better drugs.

"You're a journalist, aren't you?" he asked her.

She seemed pleased he'd heard of her, though he hadn't really. It was just that he was starting to twig: Benny had got hold of some information. His usual recourse would have been to sell it back to whoever he'd stolen it from, but that evidently wasn't the profitable option here.

Daisy looked at Benny. "Fetch us some coffees, would you?"

"They're not serving yet."

"Or you could step over the road."

He cottoned on. "Be five minutes."

When he'd left, John said, "I didn't think people were called Daisy any more."

"It's making a comeback. Are you really a spy?"

"I'm a civil servant."

"That's a spy answer. Why did you come looking for Benny?"

"It's my job. Making sure he's all right."

"Why would he need someone doing that?"

"Injured in the line of duty," John said.

"His limp."

He nodded. "What kind of journalist are you?"

"How many kinds are there?"

"They're mostly columnists these days, aren't they?"

She said, "I'm the proper kind."

"For an actual newspaper? Or just one of those websites?"

"You're not a fan of the modern world?"

"It's not a fan of me."

"Can't think why." She gave him an appraising look: too appraising, really. He wasn't sure whether this was down to her being a journalist, or just being so bloody young. She said, "But no, I work for an actual newspaper."

She named it. It was indeed big, in the sense of being a household name.

"And what's your interest in Benny?" he said.

"He has a story."

John said, "Yes, well. Everyone's got one of those."

"But Benny's is big."

"So why haven't you published it?"

"There are details to be ironed out."

"Such as?"

"Well, Benny wants more money than my editor wants to give him. And my editor wants proof that it's actually true."

"Inconvenient things like that. What's the story?"

Daisy said, "Ah, you nearly had me there. I nearly gave it away."

"I thought when you people were working on a story with a witness like our Benny, you locked yourselves away in a motel or something. Lived on takeaways. Made sure nobody could poach your talent."

"I saw that film once. It was quite old, wasn't it?"

"Nobody's got the budget any more, have they?"

"Maybe sometimes. For a big enough story."

"And this isn't?"

"It is if it's true. But Benny has form. He approached us once before."

"'Us?'"

"The paper. Not me. It was before my time."

"And what was Benny selling then?"

"He didn't get around to saying. He had a story, he said. It involved spooks. That would be you lot."

John bowed his acknowledgement. Spooks would be his lot. Or that's what it might look to an outsider, anyway. As far as spooks were concerned, he was just a milkman. "So the story never got printed."

"The story never got printed."

And that would have been about how the Service recruited Benny for a black-books op, he thought. He must have worried he'd be left out in the cold, which was something that happened to spies, and sought an alternative form of payment just in case. Or else to encourage the Park to dig deeper. He didn't lack confidence, Benny Manors, that was for sure. A more circumspect character might have wondered how the Park would react to the squeeze being applied. But it had worked out for him in the end. And now here he was again, with another story to sell, only this time he seemed to really want to do it.

He said, "And now he's back."

"I was an intern at the time, but I was shadowing the journalist on the story. Dave Bateman?" She waited, but John offered no response. "Anyway, he's one of the best in the business, Dave. And he thought there was something there."

"Even though it never arrived."

"So when Benny turned up again, claiming he had another story, I thought, I want a piece of that."

"And Dave wasn't interested?"

"He's moved on."

Whether this was to a different paper or a different way of life entirely wasn't clear. John decided it didn't matter.

"So now you're talking to Benny. And your editor isn't sure."

Daisy said, "My editor doesn't trust Benny. Not after last time."

"And you do?"

"I think he's got a story." She put her elbow on the table, leaned her chin on her palm. "Your being here kind of proves that."

"In what way?"

"In a spy-ey way. You're here to tell me he's making it up, aren't you? That the evidence is faked."

"I don't even know what his story is, much less whether his evidence is shonky."

"So why were you looking for him?"

"Good question." He saw Benny entering with a take-away cup in his hand. "He's being looked for, though. I can tell you that much. What's the story?"

She waggled a finger. "Uh-uh."

"But something big."

"Massive."

"Except your editor isn't buying it. In every sense."

Benny arrived and put the coffee in front of Daisy. "A latte. Just the way you like it."

"I take it black."

"Oh. Looks like it's mine, then." Retrieving the cup, he looked at John. "So. He's been explaining how unhappy MI5 is about you publishing my story. I told you the spooks would be coming out of the woodwork."

"You did," agreed Daisy. "On the other hand, this one doesn't have a clue what you're selling."

They both studied John. He felt like an art exhibit.

"In fact, I'm not convinced he's a spy. He doesn't look like one."

"The best don't," John suggested, though even he wasn't convinced himself.

"So you might have put him up to it."

Benny said, "Be reasonable. If I wanted someone who looked like a spy, I'd have picked someone else. Someone with a bit charisma."

I am still here, thought John. He said, "Look," and turned to Benny. "Like I said, there are people looking for you. Spooks, yes, but they're not on Park time, they've gone freelance. And whatever you've done, whatever you've got, my guess is they want to stop you. So your best bet is to come with me. You'd be safer at the Park."

Benny threw back his head and laughed.

"I mean it. I've spoken to First Desk there."

"First Desk?" asked Daisy.

"That's what they call the chief."

"Sounds like you got that from a book."

Benny was still laughing, adding theatre by producing a tissue and wiping his eyes.

"You've made your point," Daisy told him.

"I wasn't expecting that," Benny said. "I told you they'd try to stop us. And this is what they're up to. They're hoping I'll just trot along to the Park at John here's heels. Like a bloody puppy!"

He laughed some more: an over-long solo.

"So let me get this straight," John said, once Benny had more or less finished. "You"—meaning Daisy—"think he's using me to set you up. And you"—this being Benny—"think the Park's using me to set you up."

"And how does that make you feel?" Daisy wondered.

He shrugged. "At this stage, I'm pretty used to being used. But I have to tell you, I haven't a clue what it's all about."

"Hey, Yol," said Benny. "What time do you start serving?"

"Couple of hours."

"How about you make me a present of a bottle for now, then. And I'll make you a present of some money?"

"Not the way it works, Benny," Yol told him, but even as he was saying it he was reaching under the counter for a bottle of what John could only assume was Benny's regular tipple: a bottle of Greensand Ridge gin, it turned out. He'd evidently moved on from Brown Ale.

"And three glasses," said Daisy.

Daisy said, "My problem is, my editor's problem, you've got photos, you've got audio—you've got sound and vision, basically—but these things can be faked."

"Not by me."

"I'm not saying by you. I'm saying you're the one selling. And last time you came to us with a story, well. Story never happened, did it?"

The bottle was on its last legs, but the bar had opened for business now. So far, all this meant was the door had been propped open and the summer's afternoon had peeped in. It evidently hadn't liked what it had seen. Maybe the summer's evening would be more in the mood, and stop for a cocktail. Meanwhile it was just the three of them and Yol, who'd finished his polishing and was idling behind the bar. Yol, lolling. The words made a nice little circle in John's mind, and he admired their pirouette for a while before returning to the business at hand.

He still had no idea what story Benny was trying to sell, other than—as Benny had said more than twice—it was huge. Massive. Needed to be told.

"So why not slap it on the web?"

Benny rubbed finger and thumb together. "The old do-re-mi. Can't make money out of the internet."

"Nobody says 'do-re-mi.' And Amazon seems to manage."

Benny ignored him. "I'm not a citizen journalist."

"Thank God," said Daisy.

She had drunk less than the two men, possibly because she regarded this as working. Come to think of it, John was working too. Sort of.

He said, "Where did the stuff come from, anyway? The photos and what not?"

Benny just looked at him.

"Pick them up on the job, did you?" John turned to Daisy. "Benny used to be a burglar. Did he tell you that?"

"No," Daisy said. "He did not."

"Mended my ways, didn't I?" Benny asked.

"Can't scale the walls the way he once did, mind," John said. He slapped the banquette, having aimed for his own leg. He tried again. "Old war wound."

"In the service of my country."

Daisy said, "It's an honour, really. Just sitting in the same booth."

"I need a cigarette."

"And I need a . . ." John countered. He waved a hand in the vague direction of the toilets. "Pee."

He sat in a cubicle and called Di Taverner. There was unexpectedly good reception. But then maybe a lot of business calls were made from wine bar toilets: he wouldn't know.

"You're in a bar," she told him. "Surprise surprise."

"I'm in a bar because Benny's here," he said. "I've made contact."

"And what exactly is our Benny peddling that's causing such a fuss?"

"Yes, well, I'm still working on that."

She sighed emphatically enough that he could feel as well as hear it. "Do you remember what we said about second chances? Do you recall that part of our conversation?"

"It's in hand."

"Judging by the echo, it's not the only thing in hand. Next time you give me an update, be holding more than your dick, John. It makes you look needy."

Back at the booth, Benny's cigarette had speeded up his metabolism, or slowed it down: whichever was required to make him a notch drunker than he'd been. It seemed a good moment to divide the rest of the bottle and suggest a second. There was an out-there chance he'd be able to claim it on expenses, John thought, a flash of optimism that crashed and burned when he discovered the price. Accounts would assume he'd bought a car. When he returned to the table, Benny was saying, "So your editor'll just step on it, that what you're saying? Because there are other papers out there. Other editors."

"And they'll all know we passed on it, Benny. And they'll all know why."

"None of it's faked."

"So you keep saying. And what we've seen and heard looks good. But until you tell us how you came to have hold of it, we're not prepared to accept it as kosher. So please, Benny, if you want this story heard—and believe me, I do—then fill in the gaps, and we'll take it from there."

"You don't sound drunk," John complained.

"That's because I've not been drinking. I mean, seriously, John. It's barely lunchtime."

He could have sworn he'd filled her glass at least once.
The possibility that she'd been pouring it on the floor
filled him with expensive horror.

Daisy stood. "I'm going for some fresh air. And also,
you know. Pop in to the office and that sort of thing. Why
not think it over, Benny? Maybe John can help. Flesh out
the details, and I'll run it past the paper one more time.
But we're getting short of options, okay?"

Then she was gone.

Benny reached for the bottle.

"I should probably have got her to pay for that," said
John. "Expenses."

Benny rolled his eyes. "Always a little behind the curve,
eh, John?"

He shrugged.

They continued to drink.

And then it was late afternoon, and they weren't in the wine
bar any more, but a nearby pub. There'd been some misunderstanding with Yol, John couldn't recall the details.
It might have involved payment. Benny's limp didn't get
in the way of a stand-up row, nor impede him when a
swift departure was required. Practice, John supposed. All
of this, he was more spectator than participant. Didn't stop
Yol catching him on the back of the head with a wet tea
towel on his way out.

Anyway.

For reasons of economy they'd switched from gin to beer, which increased the traffic to and from the gents. Conversation had loosened up too, ranging from the quality of the bar snacks on offer to Benny fondly recalling their first meeting, when he'd punched John in the face.

"What was it you said?"

"Leg like an overcooked noodle," John remembered. "Not that it's slowed you down much."

"I still do holiday jobs, yeah."

". . . Like a student?"

"Keep up, mate. Do I look like a fucking student?" He didn't. "When the homeowners are on holiday, that's when I do a job. Less call for the speedy getaway."

"And that's how you found this story you're selling," said John.

Benny gave him a hard stare, blurred at the edges.

"The story Daisy thinks is important, but her editor doesn't believe."

"Yes he does. Just thinks it needs . . . nailing down."

"Because you stole it," John said. "Making things tricky from a legal point of view."

"Fag break."

This time, John followed him outside. There was a gaggle of smokers there, if that was the collective noun—a chokehold? Which sounded clever, though maybe wasn't.

Benny begged a light then drew away, John following. The streets were busy, everyone enjoying a summer's evening: fun while it lasts. Tomorrow he'd feel more bruised than hungover, like he'd been dragged through a gravel pit. His mouth was numb and his pockets empty. He hated to think of the punishment he'd put his credit card through. But Benny was talking.

"Nice little score, that's all it was supposed to be."

A conversation in a pub: man who worked for a carpet-cleaning firm and had just that day completed a four-storey place in Hampstead. Family away for a fortnight. Some of the chemicals, you're best off being absent for a while.

Benny had laid a twenty on him before fading into the background.

"Some people," he said, "like the idea of getting their fingers a bit dirty. Too chickenshit to actually plunge their hands in."

Or just too law-abiding, John thought. A bit chatty down the boozer, but generally law-abiding.

"Thing is, the guy in the four-storey house? The family man? He was connected, right? Well connected. If you get my drift."

John didn't. Organised crime?

"Give you a clue, mate. A recently deceased gentleman."

John couldn't think of anyone who'd died since 2016. Nobody famous, anyway.

"Headlines?"

. . . The American, John remembered. The American billionaire. The American billionaire sex trafficker who suicided in his cell.

"Yeah, him." Benny sucked hard on his cigarette, as if he were trying to get the lit end into his mouth. "He lived over here half the time, didn't he? And that's who my man was connected to. Used to be invited to those house parties, the ones with happy endings guaranteed."

Happy endings for the fat rich men his age, thought John. Less happy for the teenage girls involved.

The beer and the gin were sloshing about inside him. He felt like a car wash.

He wasn't even sure he was still taking part in this conversation. Benny was doing all the talking.

"And of course, you know who else used to attend those parties."

John didn't.

Then he did.

Benny tapped the side of his nose with his finger. He seemed to have adopted most of his gestures from cheesy soap operas.

"H.R.H.," he said. "If you'll pardon the abbreviation."

The car wash was going into its lathering cycle. Cigarette smoke was drifting past John's face, crawling up his nose, into his mouth.

"And my man—Mr. Four-Storey—well, he had a few crafty souvenirs, didn't he?"

Audio and visual, John remembered.

"All on his laptop, handy as you like. Course, I fed that into a crusher first thing. Soon as I knew what I'd got hold of, I mean."

He put a hand in his pocket, and when he withdrew it was clutching a USB stick.

"Always with me," he said. "One and only copy."

John Bachelor turned and threw up into the gutter.

Benny stood next to him, a hand on his shoulder while he heaved.

"You're my milkman, John," he said. "Don't forget. You're here to make sure I'm all right."

"Oh God. What now?"

And here was Daisy back.

"John's been taken poorly," Benny said. "Must have been something he didn't bother to eat."

He felt better after being sick. Not brilliant, but better. And was capable of ambulatory motion—capable of constructing the phrase "ambulatory motion," even—because here he was, cutting through Holborn, the three of them like friends, Daisy one side, Benny Manors the other. Yes, friends. He hadn't had a day like this in as long as he could remember. Spending the sunshine getting wasted with his best mate, and staggering home shot to pieces. Jesus, he'd had a skinful. How much money had he got through? Best not think about that.

Daisy pulled on his arm as they reached a road. "Oi! Let's not walk under a bus, all right?"

Let's not.

He'd cleaned himself up in the loo before leaving the pub, and had managed a quick call to Di Taverner. Voicemail. So he'd left a message—nothing too revealing, but enough to let her know he'd completed his mission. And that Benny Manors carried his evidence, the *one and only copy*, on his person at all times. It was possible he'd mentioned Solly's flat, and their arrangement that he get to stay there. Anyway, that done, he'd returned to the bar to find Benny had bought another round, and it would have been rude not to drink it. Settled his stomach. That or the one after.

And now they were walking through Holborn, cutting down a back street, heading for a bus stop. And that feeling, the feeling of being with friends, wouldn't go away: it had been months, years, since he'd felt this companionship. Sure, there were clients. Mornings drinking weak tea with old men and women; hearing stories he'd heard before. Tales of courage as faded as the throws on their sofas. He didn't doubt their heroism, these wizened heroes; he just wondered what stories he'd have to tell when his time came, and whether there'd be anyone listening. Benny was saying something funny, and John hadn't caught it but laughed anyway, like friends do, and the large man who loomed out of nowhere didn't touch him hard, just rammed a forearm across his throat and the world went watery. He dropped to his knees so suddenly, something gave. And Daisy screamed, but not for long, and then she too was on the ground, everything about her out of focus. None of that took long. Benny, though; Benny was really being given the business. He was making the noises a punchbag makes. There must have been two of them, because someone was holding Benny up; he'd have been a puddle on the pavement otherwise. John stopped paying attention and threw up again. Then practised breathing. The men stopped hitting Benny and went away. More people came running towards them, shouting nothing coherent. And somewhere on the far side of London a siren was already wailing their way; would grow louder and louder until John couldn't hear it at all but was wrapped up inside it instead, a little lump of silence at the heart of a beating city.

He remained in bed for two days. Then his phone rang and wouldn't stop, and he had to crawl out to find it. Whatever they'd done to him at Casualty had stopped the pain for a while but not forever. It felt like his knee was bursting.

"You bastard. Thought that was clever, didn't you?"

"... Benny?"

His voice was a scratchy old recording; one of those Victorian wax pressings that captured starched collars and indignation, but failed to convey much meaning.

"You bastard."

John managed to haul himself onto a chair. Here, once, Solly had sat, looking at the houses opposite and imagining the lives they held, all the different possibilities crammed into a terrace. His own possibilities had ended in the room John had just emerged from.

"They took my memory."

That's what he thought Benny said, and for a moment he revelled in the idea of the same thing happening to him. Total erasure. He could start again with a blank slate, make less of a mess of things this time.

Stick, though. Benny meant memory *stick*.

His one and only copy.

John said, "I didn't know ..."

But he had really. Had known Lady Di Taverner would cause bad things to happen. You couldn't walk around with the kind of knowledge Benny had been carrying and not expect ramifications.

My man—Mr. Four-Storey—he had a few crafty souvenirs, didn't he?

H.R.H. If you'll pardon the abbreviation ...

John remembered that feeling he'd had of being with friends, walking through Holborn with Benny and Daisy, and closed his eyes. Never friends. Never friends. They'd all wanted something from the others.

And then Benny was laughing: a manic chuckle. John pictured it escaping through broken teeth and swollen lips.

"You really thought that was it, didn't you? *The one and only.* You fucking idiot."

". . . Benny?"

"Why'd you think I told you that? You think I wasn't expecting your pals to show up?"

"I didn't know, Benny. I didn't know they were coming."

"You keep telling yourself that."

". . . How's Daisy?"

"How's Daisy? Daisy's battered, isn't she? Face like an overripe melon. Still, she's feeling better about things than you are."

"What do you mean, Benny? What do you mean?"

"Like I said, I was expecting your pals to show up. And that was the clincher, wasn't it? Daisy getting a battering too, that was the cherry on top." He paused, and John heard a fizzing sound, a cigarette being lit. "No editor in the world's gonna take that lying down, are they? Someone smashes your reporter's face in—*spook heavies* smash your reporter's face in—stands to reason you've a story on your hands. A real live breathing story. Your lot think they stole the proof when they took my memory stick." Another pause for inhalation. "But that was a copy, John. I'm not a fucking fool."

"That's why you kept me drinking."

"Well it wasn't for your company, was it?"

John shook his head, though he couldn't have said why.

"So it's a happy pay day for me, and fuck you, John Bachelor. I imagine your bosses are ready to dump on you good and hard."

He didn't want to ask why, because he suspected he already knew.

"Go look at the papers, John. All of them are running it now. Every last one."

"Benny—"

"Bye bye, milkman."

And Benny laughed again, that same broken chuckle, though there was genuine mirth in it, John could tell. And it continued bouncing round his head long after the call had ended.

Oliver Nash laid the newspapers out as if he were playing solitaire. Eleven front pages. Two broadsheets, the rest tabloid. The headlines on each were much the same, as was the photograph on all but one: a figure, naked from the waist up, turning away from the camera, a salacious grin shining on his teeth. The young woman he was reaching for was also topless, her frightened eyes gazing directly at the lens. The picture on the eleventh front page was of a woman in a bikini holding a lottery card.

It was reassuring to know that some standards never wavered.

Nash said, "Well. This the sort of thing you were expecting?"

Lady Di scanned the display. It reminded her of similar situations, none of which had ended well for the subject of the photograph. Some heads rolled farther than others, of course. There was an historical precedent there which the broadsheets, at any rate, would no doubt cite in their editorials.

She said, "More or less."

He said, "The Palace has issued a denial in the strongest terms, of course. But then, it would, wouldn't it?"

"Of course."

"It's the worst crisis for the monarchy since the death of the princess."

"Yes, well, don't look at me. That was nothing to do with us."

He looked at his phone. "And the internet is going crazy. Calls for his immediate trial and imprisonment."

"The rule of law actually takes a little longer."

"Try telling that to our keyboard judiciary." He gave her a long stare. It was hard to tell whether it contained admiration. "I'm wondering whether you appreciate the scale of what you've done."

"What *I've* done?"

"The Park."

"I take instruction from our elected leaders. You know that. And Number Ten wanted this business dealt with once and for all."

He returned his gaze to the headline display. "Yes, I'm not sure this was the outcome the PM had in mind."

The PM had arguably weathered worse himself.

"And when do you pull the plug?" Nash asked.

"Twelve twenty-seven."

"Admirably precise."

"It's an operation, Oliver. We find it best to be precise. Aiming for there or thereabouts can prove woefully inadequate."

"And who gets it first?"

"The BBC."

"There's nothing like tradition, is there?"

"Well," said Lady Di. "Auntie does do these big occasions *so* well."

She glanced at her watch. Two and a half hours to go.

Nash removed one of the newspapers. "This one'll die in a ditch," he said.

"Probably."

"Shaky financial ground as it is," he said. "And once H.R.H. has sued its arse off, it'll be curtains." He shook his head. "You know, our national press has always been a guardian of our democracy. And here we are destroying its reputation for the sake of one of our, shall we say, less reputable figureheads."

She said, "It's not the first time I've green-lit an operation I'm not overwhelmingly proud of. It won't be the last. But look at the bigger picture. The Service hasn't enjoyed many favours from the present government. Any smile we can bring to its face, we'll be glad about when our budget's next considered. You of all people should think of that as good news."

"And democracy, anyway," Nash said, "isn't the PM's favourite institution." He dropped the paper. "He'll be glad to have this disappear from the news stands. Not exactly an admirer of his antics."

Diana said, "That paper bought the story from a known thief and blackmailer. Who, in turn, claims to have discovered those photographs, and the audio recordings, on a laptop stolen from a house belonging to an associate of a billionaire paedophile, an associate who does not in fact exist. The property our thief and blackmailer burgled is currently vacant, and has been for some time. And the evidence itself—the audio, the photographs—while extremely convincing, are fakes. And we can prove this because we have video footage of their being faked. Footage which everyone in the country will have seen a hundred times over by bedtime. On the BBC to start with, and then YouTube or whatever." She steepled her fingers. "After which, all further rumours about H.R.H.'s involvement with a convicted sex trafficker will be stomped on by every newspaper proprietor in the country, not to mention every editor of every TV and radio news show in the land. Goodbye nudge-nudge headlines, goodbye sniggering comments on Radio Four panel shows."

"And the attack on the journalist?"

"She was on a drunken spree with Manors. Probably planning how they'd spend the loot."

"So our version is, she was involved from the start?"

"I think that's tidiest, don't you?"

Nash said, "Manors will know he was set up. The carpet cleaner he met in the pub, who pointed him at the target house. Obviously one of us. And John Bachelor, of course. Someone he actually recognised as a spook."

"He can know all he wants. Nobody will touch him with a bargepole. As for Bachelor, he didn't have a clue what was going on. He'd have found a way to mess it up if he did. But he owed the Service rent, and all he had to do was show his face, so Manors would think we were trying to shut his story down. Which, in turn, would corroborate the whole thing as far as the press was concerned. Job done."

"And yet, and yet," said Nash. He tapped the photograph of a leering H.R.H., or someone very like him, on the nearest front page. "Some mud'll stick."

"Enough's stuck already he could start his own farm. But a lot of people will think that him being innocent of this makes him innocent of everything else he's accused of. It's worked before."

"Oh, God in heaven! Who else have you—No. Don't tell me."

"I wasn't about to." She regarded him almost fondly. "I know it doesn't sit well. But if it makes you feel better, we'll expect certain assurances. As regards future behaviour."

"Assurances," repeated Oliver Nash. "Yes, that's a comfort, isn't it? Assurances."

"It's not nothing."

"Well, you consider the source, don't you?" said Nash. "From a man of honour, no. It wouldn't be nothing."

He stacked the papers into a pile, tucked them under his arm, and left the office.

And before the day dies John Bachelor, too, has caught up with events, or at least, has learned that events have moved on without him; has switched on Solomon Dortmund's funny little television set, with its rabbit-eared aerial, and switched it off again once the news has rolled past, over and over. It seems that the story Benny Manors was anxious to sell is just that: a story. It seems that writs are descending from on high, and that lawyers all over London are rubbing their hands in glee or running for cover. It seems that rumours that have slow-cooked for a decade or more have been plated and served, and found to be foul. And it seems that John himself was party to this feast, though on whose side, and hoping for what end, he remains unsure.

Perhaps the peach brandy will clarify matters. But for the moment all he has is a painful knee and a sore throat, and a mind that can't keep up with itself.

He wonders about Benny and Daisy, and how they will fare in the face of this reversal. (He will not have to wonder long. *Partners in slime* will read one headline the following morning. *Devious pair plot to destroy Prince's reputation.* And Daisy's bruised and battered face will grace many pages, next to an old mugshot of Benny Manors, current whereabouts unknown.) Mostly, though, out of habit and fear, he wonders about his own situation, and how bad it will turn out to be. And again, he will not be left long in limbo: soon the phone will ring, and it will be Diana Taverner, or if not Lady Di, someone tasked by her with making a tiresome call. Is he John Bachelor? He is. Is he currently residing at blah blah, blah blah, blah blah? Yes, and yes, and yes. In which case, he is hereby informed that his presence at such address is illegal and unwarranted and shall cease forthwith. Keys to be surrendered. Absence to be swift and permanent.

As for his role in the Service, and its continuation or otherwise . . .

Well. He will find out soon enough.

Through the window the rest of London looms, large and devoid of welcome. The more he stares the darker it grows; and larger too, by the minute.

But at least there is still brandy in the bottle, he thinks.

Though in this, he is mistaken.

Continue reading for a preview of

THIS IS WHAT HAPPENED

1

The longer she sat there, the colder she became. With her back to the cistern, and her feet drawn up beneath her, Maggie perched on the closed lid of the toilet, and concentrated on being as still as possible. An hour earlier, a spasm in her leg had caused the overhead lights to switch on. Their electric hum had startled her more than the glare. Someone would hear it, she thought, and come investigate. But nobody arrived, and the spasm subsided, and a few minutes later the lights turned themselves off again.

"How long do I have to hide in the toilets?" she had asked Harvey.

"Until twelve. At least."

"The guard patrols all night long."

"But there's only one of him. And he can't be on every floor at once."

She had an urge to confirm that the flash drive was still in her pocket, but any movement would bring the lights to life, and besides, she had checked three times already.

Alone in the dark Maggie squeezed her eyes shut, tried not to shiver, and made herself invisible.

Quilp House was twenty-seven storeys high, each spreading out from a central lobby area where the lifts were, and around which the stairwells ran. In the lower half of the building the floors were open-plan, with rows of desks divided into three or four work-stations apiece. During the day a kind of electricity filled the air, which was not so much the ambient excitement caused by communion with the world's markets as much as it was the repressed emotions of people forced to work in close proximity, and thus hold in their baser reactions, their bodily rumblings.

From the twentieth level, the building changed character. Here, people worked behind closed doors, in progressively larger offices. Views became spectacular. The higher up you were, the further off you could see the weather.

On these floors cameras blinked at corridors' ends, little red lights above their lenses signalling vigilance. Occasionally they swivelled, redirecting their meerkat gaze.

"What about the CCTV?"

"There are two guards on the night shift," Harvey had explained. He was patient with her. Without having to be told, she knew he understood what it was to step across the lines that bordered daily behaviour. "One to patrol, and the other to watch the screens. The TV monitors. Do you know how many of these there are?"

She had a vision of a wall built of pixels, boasting as many views of corridors as there were satellite channels screening sport.

"There are six," he said. "And they alternate from camera to camera. Which means the odds are against your showing up on screen at any given time."

"So they don't automatically detect motion?"

"Maggie." He had reached across the table and put his hand on hers. Around them had been the usual clatter of young mums and earnest hipsters: like most of their conversations, this had taken place in the café where they first met. Where he had first approached her. "It's fine to be scared. It's fine not to want to do this."

"I do want to do it."

"And I wouldn't ask if I could see any other way of getting the job done. If you knew—"

He broke off while a young woman squeezed past with a tray piled high with dirty mugs, their rims laced with froth.

"I know you wouldn't," she told him.

Because she was his only hope.

Her wristwatch pinged when midnight struck.

For a moment, the sound confused her—she had not

been asleep, precisely, but had entered a fugue state in which memories and plans collided, throwing sparks off each other—and she jerked upright, banging her head against the cistern. An image of her sister popped and vanished as the cubicle light flickered on, followed by the other bulbs in the lavatory. Her heart pounded. Someone would come. But nobody did, and after a moment Maggie unfolded her limbs, which were creaky with cold, and tried to rub life into them.

Pins and needles assaulted her fingers. She did not feel like an agent on a mission. She felt like a young woman up past bedtime, who wanted only to crawl beneath some covers and find warmth.

"What do I do now, Harvey?" she whispered.

It would have been nice if he'd been there, offering an answer. But it was up to her now. She was on her own.

Because it didn't matter—because the lights had blinked on anyway—before making her way out of the cubicle, she raised the toilet lid, pulled down her jeans and pants, and used it for the purpose for which it was intended. Then she rearranged her clothing, closed the lid, and had her hand on the handle before she caught herself—that would be all she needed, to send a watery alarm cascading through the building. She imagined security guards stomping up and down the stairwells, crashing into the lavatories on each floor, throwing open doors, looking for the culprit.

"Maggie, Maggie," she murmured to herself.

When her heart rate was normal she unlocked her cubicle and tiptoed to the door and opened it and peered out.

The corridor was in darkness. The motion sensors were sleepy, and wouldn't kick in until she stepped outside. Even then they allowed a second or two's grace, as if they needed convincing that they weren't rousing themselves for someone of no consequence. For a mouse, creeping its night-time way along an empty hall.

Rather than a spy. An agent on a mission.

"Trying not to make the lights come on will only stress you out," Harvey had said. "It can't be done. You have to move to get where you need to be, and the sensors will do the rest. So don't worry about them. You can't control the things you can't control."

It was nice that he was confident she could control the other things.

"Maggie, Maggie," she chided herself again. Here was the equation: if the lights were off, the guard wasn't on this floor. And if he wasn't on this floor, he wouldn't see the lights coming on.

Which meant it was safe to step out into the corridor.

But before she could do so the lights flickered and the door to the lobby clicked shut, and then—loud as a lion— she could hear the breathy whistling of the security guard as he rounded the corner, heading her way.

"**I wish** this were like the films," Harvey had said, "where you have an earpiece and a radio mic, and we're synchronised to the nanosecond. And I'd be hacked into the security system, so I could tell you when it's safe to walk down a corridor, and when to shelter under a desk. But life's not like that, Maggie. This business isn't like that. We're a lot more . . . We're less James Bond and a lot more, I don't know, Mr. Bean or someone. We have to use what's at hand. And I wish I didn't have to ask you to do this. If I could do it myself, I would. If there were any other way . . ."

He had not finished his sentence. He hadn't needed to.

"And let me say this. You're a brave girl, a tremendous girl, and I couldn't be prouder of you. But if you want to back out, do it now. Because from here on, it'll be too late."

"I don't want to back out."

She did, though.

What he was asking was that she put her head in the dragon's mouth. It was so far removed from her daily life she might as well be watching it in one of those films it wasn't like, and even there at the table she could feel her innards contract, her thighs grow watery. She'd wobble when she stood, she knew she would. And she ought to tell him he'd picked the wrong girl, a nobody, who couldn't be relied on. She'd dissolve into panic at the worst moment. She wasn't icy cool and she wasn't super-hot. He'd plucked her from a crowd, and really, it would be sensible to let her subside back into it, and lose herself among the traffic.

But if she said that she'd see disappointment cross his features, that strange mix of the ugly and the sad on which she'd come to depend.

And besides … And besides, what he was asking of her was important. For Queen and country, he'd have said in the old days, though here in the modern world it was more tangible than that. What he was asking her to be was a cog in a larger wheel, on whose turning much depended. He was giving her the opportunity of helping ensure that something did not happen. That there was a fundamental anonymity to this—success measured as an absence of event—did not faze her. Anonymity was her natural setting, her personality's screensaver. Just ask Meredith.

"Good, then. Good." He fished about in his pocket.

For all he'd said about not being James Bond, Maggie had still expected something flashy, in a silver case perhaps, moulded to fit. But instead he'd handed her a very ordinary flash drive, the size of her thumb. It was black, with a white label so its contents could be indexed. This was blank, of course. When she reached to take it from him, he held it over her palm for a moment.

"But listen. Whatever happens, you mustn't let this fall into their hands. They mustn't know you've got it, mustn't know you've used it. Once it's done its job, you have to either get it out of the building, or hide it somewhere it won't be found. And they will be look-ing." His gaze was intense. She imagined this the look men used when sending other men to war. *You might not come back. But I will remember you.* "If they find you, if they know you've been there, they'll be looking for this. And they mustn't find it. I can't tell you how crucial that is."

"I understand."

"Do you?"

She could only nod.

He let go of the drive and there it was, on her palm.

Maggie made a fist round it, keeping it safe.

She melted back inside, letting the door close silently, and stood with her back to it, her heart's hammering the loudest sound in London. He would hear her through the wood, and see the light beneath the door. Or put a hand to it and push, the automatic gesture of the guard on patrol, and when he encountered the resistance of her weight, it would be over. Alarms would sound, or whistles blow. Those meerkat cameras would turn and point, and her image would plaster itself over the monitors down-stairs—six of them? The other guard, the one whose job it was to lean back in his chair and eat doughnuts, would reach for the telephone. And it would not be the police he would call, Harvey had left her in no doubt about that. The people whose building this was, whose secrets it contained, they looked after their own. The last thing they'd do would be call the police.

But he won't see the light, she thought, because the lights are on in the corridor too. There'll be no telltale yellow strip painting the carpet. This was just another door, the ladies' loo, and why would he check that it opened? It always opened.

His whistling was familiar, a tune on the edge of her recall. It faded as he walked past, and the creaking of his tread on the carpet disappeared. The door he'd come through, from the lobby where the lifts and stairwells were, was off to her right, and if he completed a circuit of the floor he would not pass by again but enter the same lobby from the other side. But she didn't know his routines, whether he might halt halfway and retrace his steps, or whether he was heading for a particular desk, or for the vending machine in the kitchen area . . . She could slip out now, and run into him three seconds later. Or this might be as close as their paths would come, and the fact that she'd just evaded him—had all but felt his breath on her cheek—might itself be a token that her safety was now assured.

Maggie, Maggie . . .

There were no tokens, no guarantees. But what was certain was that the light was currently on. Slipping into the corridor would cause nothing to change. As soon as this thought took hold of her she acted on it, standing upright, opening the door, stepping outside. The corridor was empty. Choosing the direction the guard had come from, she hurried round the corner to the lobby door.

She had spent hours in the toilet on the eighteenth floor. This was seven flights below where she needed to be, but that had been planned for—had been her own idea.

"If they catch me—"

(An outcome that had to be acknowledged.)

"—if I'm caught, at least they won't know what I was really after."

"You're a natural." Harvey's ugly face broadened when he smiled, and the tips of his incisors showed. He had a high forehead, a receding hairline, and while his hair was clipped short, it had a noticeable curl, and left to itself would probably fall into ringlets. It was a light dirty brown in colour. He favoured open-necked shirts with a check pattern, and in cold weather wore a long black overcoat with a wide collar, of a kind she could imagine adorning gangsters. "You've done this before—admit it!"

He joked to put her at her ease, and it worked.

So now she was in the lobby of the eighteenth, and needed to climb seven storeys.

The doors required a security pass. She wore hers on a lanyard round her neck, and flashed it now across the face of the reader, which blinked red to green and allowed her through. The stairwell had no windows, and the lights were constantly on, a health and safety requirement. But the stairs were uncarpeted, and difficult to climb noiselessly. They made her trainers squeak. She tried to step only on the runners, two at a time, but still foot and stair conspired to produce this noise, like a cat's toy. If he reached the stairwell again—or so much as put his head round the door—he'd hear her. What good would speed do her then? Better to climb slowly, hugging the wall, out of the line of sight. She was just about to do this when a door, some flights below, opened.

"Remember, the building won't be empty."

"Even after midnight?"

Every so often a look would ripple across his face, like the shadow of a cloud, and in it she could see irritation, frustration—disappointment, mostly. She was adept at the art of reading disappointment. And when that happened it was as if a fish-hook tugged at her heart.

But Harvey had not let his feelings break surface.

"There'll always be someone. Not on the upper floors, but lower down, where the actual work gets done. You know, by ordinary people. Like you and me."

He was not ordinary. But she was, and this was the obstacle she had to overcome.

"The markets sleep for no man," he said. "But you should be okay. Overnighters are for junior staff. The top floors will be quiet. All the fat cats'll be home in their little palaces, or snuggling their mistresses in five-star hotels."

He'd actually said *snuggling*. The word distracted her from any number of questions, complaints really, worries—such as, What if I'm spotted? What do I say when I'm challenged? What if I'm caught in the stairwell, and someone shouts up at me:

"Hello?"

Tight against the wall, she tried to make herself smaller.

"Anyone there?"

She didn't move.

For what felt like a minute, nothing happened. Perhaps he had been convinced by her pretended absence. The only way of being sure was to lean forward and see him not seeing her, but to do so would break that spell. But if he came up the stairs to check, if he found her trying to hide—

Another door opened. The one Maggie had come through.

"Sir?"

A deep voice, a bass delight. The security guard.

"Oh, Joshua, hi—thought I heard someone."

"Just doing the rounds, sir."

"Yeah, you don't need to call me that—how you doing, anyway? All good?"

"All fine, sir."

Maggie recognised the rhythm of the exchange. A young man in a suit, and another in a uniform. White/black went without saying.

The younger man, the suit, came up a flight, so the two were only one level apart.

"You still turning out on a Saturday?"

Maggie heard a rustling kind of noise, as if he were miming something physical, the throwing of a ball, the wielding of a bat.

". . . Sir?"

"The old rugger?"

"I don't play rugby, sir."

"Oh, right, no, only I thought—"

"Don't go for sports at all, sir."

"Right. Must be thinking of someone else, yeah?"

"Sir."

"Well, I'd better be . . . Have a good night, Josh."

"You too, sir."

A door opened, closed.

Maggie's palms, flat against the wall, felt wet as well as cold.

"The old rugger," the security guard said.

After a moment, another door opened and closed, and she was alone in the stairwell once more.

When she was ready to move, Maggie crept up the remaining flights. She kept her back to the wall, and allowed time for her trainers' squeaks to subside between each step. It reminded her of being a teen again, slinking to her bedroom after a night spent with Jezza, desperate not to make a sound, knowing that the slightest creak would wake her parents' wrath.

At the twenty-fifth floor she let herself into the lobby.

Before the lights came on, there were men in each corner, four of them, waiting—a trap. But when the now-familiar flickering to life was done, the men turned into pot plants, their thick green leaves like rubbery imploring hands. Instead of earth, the pots were rim-full of smooth stones, between which, she imagined, each plant's roots twined and clutched. Low-maintenance vitality.

She took the right-hand door. There were offices here, but glass-walled, and she could see through them to the outside world—London after dark was a fairground whose wheels kept turning. Sleek buildings, already higher than they had a right to be, strained further skywards still, while in the spaces between them cranes clustered, resembling huge metal birds, building nests where the city allowed.

The streets were different at night too. Were colder, damper, and those who asked you for change did so in tones more aggressive than suppliant. The daylight hours taught them to know their place, and know it they did, and it was here, and now.

But she had a job to do. And once she was back on the street, Harvey would be waiting for her, bearing the thanks of a grateful Intelligence Service.

The office she was looking for was the largest on the floor, a corner suite. Ahead of her, the lights buzzed to life, and she knew that if she were observing this building from across the road, a story would be telling itself, one in which a lone woman—probably a cleaner—made her way through the night, scattering darkness as she went. But no one would guess her real mission. The door was not locked. She entered the room. *It will take two minutes, no more.* Harvey's promise. Before the lights had time to turn themselves off, she would be on her way back to the stairwell. She approached the desk, on which a laptop sat, locked to its docking device with a chain sleeved in plastic. *Two minutes.* She reached into her pocket for the flash drive.

It was gone.

Whatever happens*, you mustn't let this fall into their hands.*

She went through her pockets again—all of them. Even the ones the drive had never been in.

They mustn't find it. I can't tell you how crucial that is.

In her throat, a rising tide. It would all overcome her now, this mission she'd been chosen for, its importance, her own inconsequence. She could run away, hide under her bed, let the world go on without her. Except that that's precisely what it would do, wouldn't it? If she ran now, and failed in her mission, then the things Harvey had warned her about would happen, and the world would turn for the worse.

Once it's done its job, you have to either get it out of the building, or hide it somewhere it won't be found.

It hadn't done its job yet, and it was still in the building. It must have fallen from her pocket, would be on the stairwell, or somewhere between this office door and the lobby, or else—

The toilet.

There, where she'd crouched for hours, waiting for the office block to grow quiet and dim. She'd all but frozen in place, and even now her arms and legs felt heavy. But before leaving she'd had a pee, and that must have been when it happened, must have been when the flash drive wriggled free from her pocket. How could she not have heard it? But that was a useless thread to follow. For now, the choice was stark. She could return to the lavatory on the eighteenth floor, or . . .

Or the world would turn for the worse.

Maggie left the office. For no sensible reason she ran in a half-crouch along the corridor, as if that silent watcher in the neighbouring building weren't simply following her story but preparing to pick her off with a high-powered rifle. But the watcher didn't exist. She was alone, and hadn't been found yet, but she had no right to be here, and there was a guard on a floor below, and more people below that. All these nervy thoughts made her clumsy—at the door to the lobby her lanyard caught on a button, and in a brief slapstick routine she tugged its catch loose and her security pass fell to the floor. She bent to collect it and, as she straightened up, saw through the lobby door's porthole window the lift opening, and a man stepping out.

Once through the door, he stopped.

Was he sniffing the air, like a dog, for strangers?

Maggie had scrambled round the corner. She was now in a break-out area, so called, as if it were from here that workers might make their escape: an area three metres square, surrounded by high-backed sofas. She was lying on one in case he dropped to the floor and scanned for visible feet. Though it was more likely that he would simply walk past and see, not just her feet, but all of her, one whole young woman, twenty-six, very scared.

She closed her eyes, that ancient trick. *I can't see you, you can't see me.*

Harvey, what do I do now?

The man was talking. That same bass delight she'd heard in the stairwell. Joshua, the guard.

"Yo, yeah, I'm on twenny-five."

crackle

"No, it's juss, lights are on, man. Like something triggered them?"

crackle

"Pussy yourself, man. Doing a job here."

crackle

"Yeah, well, you get tired watching TV, we can always swap."

The crackling stopped.

Joshua paused.

He's by the pigeonholes, thought Maggie.

She knew those pigeonholes well.

And if he was by the pigeonholes, he was standing not far from where she lay. Might even be staring in her direction. If he had X-ray vision, she was caught already. And if she made a sound, a squeak, a rustle ... She was trying not to breathe. To make herself smaller than small.

The floor creaked. He'd taken a step.

Towards her?

It was like a thought experiment. Any move she made to determine his whereabouts would give her own away.

Another creak.

Was that one closer?

The sofa was red, though this didn't matter. Of the other three, another was also red, and the remaining pair were blue. Big bright bold shades. There'd have been a meeting and someone would have passed round a catalogue and a vote would have been taken. Unless there was an underlying protocol which overrode democracy—a corporate livery, a company style. This didn't matter either.

All that mattered was that she was curled up on the world's reddest sofa, whose tall back was the only thing shielding her from—

crackle

"Yo."

crackle

"Sweet, man, yeah, maybe a mouse. You know I put them traps down? The humane ones? Catch and release, right?"

The planet shifted, and if she hadn't already put a hand to her mouth, wasn't already biting down on her out-stretched index finger, she'd have screamed.

He had turned and was leaning against her sofa. The back of his head had swum into her ken, a shaved and cratered moon.

"I'll release it I catch it all right. Release it from the window. Twenny-five floors, see if the little fucker lands on its feet."

crackle

"So yeah. Kettle on. See you in ten."

She could not breathe. She could not move. She could swear she could feel his heat.

Could smell the odour of smoked cigarettes.

The sofa moved again, crawled half an inch across the floor, and seemed to vibrate at the same time—what was he doing, was he toying with her?

Catch and release.

This was what cats did, they played with their food.

And then her heart flipped as he let out a huge sigh:

"... Aaaaaaaaaaaaaaaaahhhhhhhhhhhhhhhhhhh ..."

When Maggie realised what he was doing, that he was using the sofa's high back as a scratching post, she had to bite down on her finger again, this time to keep hysteria in. A big burly man, and he was giving it a real jiggle, reaching those places his own hands never could. It must feel so great, it must feel so grand, but oh God, what if he came round to push the sofa back into place when he was done? There she'd be, curled up like his special treat, and all he'd have to do was reach out and pluck her.

It didn't happen. The sofa stopped moving as he finished his scratch and then he was gone, back the way he'd come. She lay there while he, presumably, checked the nearest offices, their glass frontages making it unnecessary for him to step inside, and then she was hearing the lobby door open and close, after which there was only silence.

Five minutes later, maybe less, the lights went out.

Harvey, you should have been there.

She wanted to make herself happy, to turn this into an anecdote.

It was like being trapped up a tree, only the bear can't see you. And all it wants to do is rub its back against the bark.

But it wasn't working. Joshua was gone, yes, but she was still here, and the flash drive still seven floors below, in the ladies' loo—she hoped—and there was nothing funny about any of it. Maybe one day. Maybe when she was in a wine bar, and Harvey was pouring the last of the second bottle into her big glass. Then it would be funny. But not yet.

The seconds ticked by, followed slowly by the minutes. She wondered if it were true, if there were mice in the building, and with the thought came a phantom tickle up her thigh, and she yelped and slapped at her leg—couldn't help it—and the lights came on.

Which was, as it were, a wake-up call. Maggie stood and clenched her fists and hurried to the door. Let herself through to the lifts, whose numbers showed that three were at ground level, the other on the twelfth. This was as much a guarantee of safety she was going to get. Out on the stairwell the air felt colder, so much so her breath was visible. She counted the steps down: twelve per half-flight. One hundred and sixty eight in all.

On the eighteenth floor, all was quiet. There were no potted plants here, though, and it struck her she'd never noticed this before. At night, you have different eyes. Different details shuffle into view.

In the ladies', everything was as she'd left it. The door to the third cubicle hung open and the toilet lid was down. The automatic freshener had spritzed the air, and a tang of artificial pine prickled her senses, but on the floor there was nothing—no flash drive—and her heart slumped inside her.

Whatever happens . . .

Where was it?

. . . you mustn't let this fall into their hands.

If not here, where?

She'd have seen it on the stairs if that's where she'd dropped it. It would not have been possible to miss a thumb-sized wedge of plastic . . . This was the process her mind was going through, a logical one-step/two-step that, followed to its destination, would restore everything to how it ought to be, and leave her triumphant, the flash drive in her palm. But her body had ideas of its own, and even now was forcing her onwards, one extra step, beyond that final cubicle to the wash-space, where the basins lined the wall. And there, in the centre of the floor, having scuttled under the partition, lay the flash drive. It was with a peculiar sense of calm and rightness that she bent to retrieve it. All that panic, Maggie, and where did it get you? Just an unnecessary shock, when if you'd gone about things in a methodical way, you'd be out of the building by now.

It was time to take a grip. Drive firmly in hand, she left the toilets and headed up the stairs again. The lights on the twenty-fifth were still on, her recent presence still eddying the air. In the corner office she knelt by the desk, unfolded the flash drive so its male part was showing, and inserted it into its port. Then turned the computer on.

"**What will** it do?"

Harvey had looked at her thoughtfully, weighing up, she assumed, the exact degree of her right to know.

And if he had refused to say, would it have made a difference? She had come this far, after all—had allowed herself to be recruited. This might have made others bridle. Made them feel used. But being used was being shown that you were useful. And Maggie wanted to be useful.

Besides, he had already told her so much, so much.

"The company is not what it claims to be," for instance.

And: "If you could be part of something huge—something life-savingly important—what risk would you be willing to run?"

Nobody would know, of course. That had been clear from the start. The heroism he was offering was anonymous, deniable, and might even be deemed criminal if things went wrong.

Turning it over and over in his mind, the way she was turning the flash drive over in her hand.

"It will install a surveillance program into the company's network."

". . . That's all?"

"It's enough, believe me."

He had a halting way of speaking, a verbal dawdle that became more pronounced when he was at his most earnest.

"It will allow us to monitor all their internal communications."

"Can't you do that anyway?"

"Theoretically, yes. But not without using a much wider net. And that means bringing in GCHQ, and that means . . . I'm sorry, Maggie. We're outside your need to know here."

She said, "You're worried that the more people know, the more chance there is of someone leaking the operation."

"Maggie . . ."

"You're worried there's a traitor in your organisation."

He glanced around.

"Nobody's listening, Harvey."

She felt like they'd just swapped shoes—here she was, reassuring him. But they were talking quietly, and the café was its usual mid-morning mayhem. Infants in their carriages and mothers on their phones. They'd have more chance of being overheard if they'd been using semaphore.

Harvey said, "Certain operational . . . weaknesses have come to light. Which make this a particularly . . . sensitive matter."

"Which is why you need me."

He smiled that gently ugly smile of his. "Which is why I need you."

The drive weighed nothing. Weighed less than a snowflake.

"So I . . ."

"You plug it into the USB port, then turn the computer on."

"I'll need a password."

"Nope. You just wait until you're prompted for one. Then power down, and then remove the drive. Couldn't be simpler."

It was safe in her grip. Safe in her hand.

Couldn't be simpler.

The screen asked for a password, in that officious way screens had.

Maggie was tempted to key a retort, *Ha ha, screw you*, but had visions of a net dropping from the ceiling, of bells going off. To have come this far to get snatched now, well. That would be . . . disappointing.

She held the power button down until the machine emitted its yelp, then closed the lid, pulled the flash drive free, and put it in her pocket.

Job done.

All that remained to do was leave.

She took a glance round the office before doing so. The view through the windows aside, it looked ordinary, as if no grim business were conducted here. The desk, the furniture, the two armchairs posed around the glass-topped coffee table, were unassumingly anonymous. The art on the wall had been chosen not to draw the eye. She had a vision of whoever it was did business behind this desk, a blank-faced man, a featureless woman, with a circular face and an inked-in nose. And then she blinked it away, and headed for the lobby.

For a moment, she considered summoning the lift and dropping twenty-five floors in one fell swoop, marching past the front desk with a wave. Harvey was waiting for her down the road. He'd be standing on a corner, their appointed rendezvous, checking his watch. *My clever girl*, he'd call her, or something. Job done. Job done.

But the lift would be a mistake, a change of gear she had no business making. Careful steps had got her this far, and careful steps would see her home. She let herself back into the stairwell. Twenty-five flights, fifty sets of stairs. There was a rhythm waiting in them, and her feet found it soon enough, just at that tipping point between speed and safety. When Maggie looked down she couldn't see the ground floor, and when she looked up couldn't see the roof. Caught between two extremes, so much the opposite of her real life, she might as well have stepped, not into a stairwell, but through the back of a wardrobe.

There'd be time for thoughts like this later. For now what mattered was these remaining flights, fifteen of them, fourteen and a half. Fourteen.

On the thirteenth floor, where else, the door opened, and she all but ran into his arms.

"Miss?" he said.

"Oh," she said. She came to a halt. Vocabulary failed her. "Oh."

"Can I ask what you're doing here, miss?"

"I was just . . . on my way home."

"But you shouldn't be up here, should you, miss?" Joshua tilted his big head to one side. "Not this time of night. I know you, though. I know you, right?"

"I work here," she said, fumbling her security pass free.

He clicked his fingers. "I do know you," he said. "You work in the post room."

". . . That's right."

"You work in the post room," he repeated. "But you shouldn't be here now."

"No, I was going home."

"Yes, miss," he said. "But you'd better come with me first. Just while we straighten this out."

Other Titles in the Soho Crime Series

Stephanie Barron
(Jane Austen's England)
*Jane and the Twelve Days
of Christmas
Jane and the Waterloo Map*

F.H. Batacan
(Philippines)
Smaller and Smaller Circles

James R. Benn
(World War II Europe)
*Billy Boyle
The First Wave
Blood Alone
Evil for Evil
Rag & Bone
A Mortal Terror
Death's Door
A Blind Goddess
The Rest Is Silence
The White Ghost
Blue Madonna
The Devouring
Solemn Graves
When Hell Struck Twelve*

Cara Black
(Paris, France)
*Murder in the Marais
Murder in Belleville
Murder in the Sentier
Murder in the Bastille
Murder in Clichy
Murder in Montmartre
Murder on the
Ile Saint-Louis
Murder in the
Rue de Paradis
Murder in the Latin Quarter
Murder in the Palais Royal
Murder in Passy
Murder at the
Lanterne Rouge
Murder Below
Montparnasse
Murder in Pigalle*

Cara Black cont.
*Murder on the
Champ de Mars
Murder on the Quai
Murder in Saint-Germain
Murder on the Left Bank
Murder in Bel-Air*

Lisa Brackmann
(China)
*Rock Paper Tiger
Hour of the Rat
Dragon Day

Getaway
Go-Between*

Henry Chang
(Chinatown)
*Chinatown Beat
Year of the Dog
Red Jade
Death Money
Lucky*

Barbara Cleverly
(England)
*The Last Kashmiri Rose
Strange Images of Death
The Blood Royal
Not My Blood
A Spider in the Cup
Enter Pale Death
Diana's Altar

Fall of Angels
Invitation to Die*

Colin Cotterill
(Laos)
*The Coroner's Lunch
Thirty-Three Teeth
Disco for the Departed
Anarchy and Old Dogs
Curse of the Pogo Stick
The Merry Misogynist
Love Songs from
a Shallow Grave
Slash and Burn*

Colin Cotterill cont.
*The Woman Who
Wouldn't Die
Six and a
Half Deadly Sins
I Shot the Buddha
The Rat Catchers' Olympics
Don't Eat Me
The Second Biggest Nothing*

Garry Disher
(Australia)
*The Dragon Man
Kittyhawk Down
Snapshot
Chain of Evidence
Blood Moon
Whispering Death
Signal Loss

Wyatt
Port Vila Blues
Fallout

Bitter Wash Road
Under the Cold Bright Lights*

David Downing
(World War II Germany)
*Zoo Station
Silesian Station
Stettin Station
Potsdam Station
Lehrter Station
Masaryk Station

(World War I)
Jack of Spies
One Man's Flag
Lenin's Roller Coaster
The Dark Clouds Shining
Diary of a Dead Man
on Leave*

Agnete Friis
(Denmark)
*What My Body Remembers
The Summer of Ellen*

Seichō Matsumoto
(Japan)
*Inspector Imanishi
Investigates*

Magdalen Nabb
(Italy)
*Death of an Englishman
Death of a Dutchman
Death in Springtime
Death in Autumn
The Marshal and
the Murderer
The Marshal and
the Madwoman
The Marshal's Own Case
The Marshal Makes
His Report
The Marshal
at the Villa Torrini
Property of Blood
Some Bitter Taste
The Innocent
Vita Nuova
The Monster of Florence*

Fuminori Nakamura
(Japan)
*The Thief
Evil and the Mask
Last Winter, We Parted
The Kingdom
The Boy in the Earth
Cult X*

Stuart Neville
(Northern Ireland)
*The Ghosts of Belfast
Collusion
Stolen Souls
The Final Silence
Those We Left Behind
So Say the Fallen*

(Dublin)
Ratlines

Rebecca Pawel
(1930s Spain)
*Death of a Nationalist
Law of Return
The Watcher in the Pine
The Summer Snow*

Kwei Quartey
(Ghana)
*Murder at Cape
Three Points
Gold of Our Fathers
Death by His Grace*

Qiu Xiaolong
(China)
*Death of a Red Heroine
A Loyal Character Dancer
When Red Is Black*

James Sallis
(New Orleans)
*The Long-Legged Fly
Moth
Black Hornet
Eye of the Cricket
Bluebottle
Ghost of a Flea*

Sarah Jane

John Straley
(Sitka, Alaska)
*The Woman Who
Married a Bear
The Curious Eat Themselves
The Music of What Happens
Death and the Language
of Happiness
The Angels Will Not Care
Cold Water Burning
Baby's First Felony*

(Cold Storage, Alaska)
*The Big Both Ways
Cold Storage, Alaska*

Akimitsu Takagi
(Japan)
*The Tattoo Murder Case
Honeymoon to Nowhere
The Informer*

Helene Tursten
(Sweden)
*Detective Inspector Huss
The Torso
The Glass Devil
Night Rounds
The Golden Calf
The Fire Dance
The Beige Man
The Treacherous Net
Who Watcheth
Protected by the Shadows*

*Hunting Game
Winter Grave*

*An Elderly Lady Is Up to
No Good*

**Janwillem van de
Wetering**
(Holland)
*Outsider in Amsterdam
Tumbleweed
The Corpse on the Dike
Death of a Hawker
The Japanese Corpse
The Blond Baboon
The Maine Massacre
The Mind-Murders
The Streetbird
The Rattle-Rat
Hard Rain
Just a Corpse at Twilight
Hollow-Eyed Angel
The Perfidious Parrot
The Sergeant's Cat:
Collected Stories*

Jacqueline Winspear
(1920s England)
*Maisie Dobbs
Birds of a Feather*